Love's Embrace

By: Mary Reason Theriot

Dedication

Without the love and support of my family and friends, I would not have pursued this new path in life. I would especially like to thank those who have proofread copy after copy, to give me their honest opinion of the books.

To my daughter, Theresa, thank you so much for your continued encouragement.

To my wonderful husband Malwen, your continued love and support mean the world to me. I don't know what I would do without you in my life. All of my books would not be what they were without you pushing me forward.

To my fans, I would like to offer a special thank you for your continued support.

ISBN-10: 1-945393-24-6
ISBN-13: 978-1-945393-24-2

Also Available by Mary Reason Theriot:

The Hideaway
The Traveler
Dr. Frankenstein
Above Suspicion
Horror in the Night
Deadly Seduction
Echoes on the Bayou
Seven Deadly Sins
A Kiss so Deadly
A Deadly Combination
CarnEvil of Souls
Seduced by Voodoo
www.maryreasontheriot.com

Prologue

Five Years Ago

A very excited Alexis Bertrand, Lexi for short, burst into her best friend's office. Startled, Kyle DuPont looked up from his desk, surprised to see her. "Is something wrong?"

Instead of answering him, she rushed over and gave him a huge hug. "I am so happy that I couldn't wait to tell you."

Kyle knew he would not get a word in edgewise when Lexi was like this. She could not keep secrets, and he could tell that she was bursting to tell him something big. Holding out her left hand, she asked, "Do you notice anything different?"

"What? Did you do your nails?"

Slapping at his arm, she laughed, "No silly." Pointing to her finger, she exclaimed, "Look! Bennett asked me to marry him."

The ground opened up underneath him. He had talked to Bennett last night, and he never mentioned proposing to Lexi. He gazed at the diamond ring as it glistened from the lights in his office. "I guess congratulations are in order then. I didn't realize the two of you were that serious."

For a moment, anger consumed him at the mere thought of someone marrying his best friend. His mouth tensed and the little vein at his temple throbbed.

As children, they chased each other, played hide and seek, and created memories while getting into plenty of mischief.

As teenagers Lexi and Kyle had become inseparable, walking to and from school together every day, having sleepovers, and taking care of each other into adulthood.

After graduating high school, they were ready to conquer the world.

Recently, he discovered he had feelings for her that he could not explain. When he looked into her eyes, he saw that they sparkled more than the ring on her finger. She was ecstatic about marrying Bennett.

Dancing around his office, she shrieked, "I know. I was so surprised when Bennett proposed. I never thought he would ask."

"So, I take it you love each other?"

Smiling over at him, she shyly replied, "More than I ever imagined. I know Bennett will want to tell you, but you are my best friend and I couldn't wait to share the news with you."

The ringing of his office phone interrupted their conversation. "I didn't mean to interrupt your work. We can get together over drinks to discuss everything."

She sailed out of his office just as fast as she had swept in, and he felt as if someone had sucker punched him in the stomach. He should be happy for his best friends, but he was overwhelmed by feelings of unexplained loss.

Chapter 1

Present Day

The Regency had once been a grand hotel in Springport, Louisiana. The impressive hotel sat on a five-acre site that overlooked the majestic Mississippi River. It housed three hundred rooms, two swimming pools, and a convention center. When it originally opened, it immediately became the place for movie stars to stay when filming in the area. Back in 1972, the presidential suite was rumored to go for two hundred dollars a night while the regular rooms started at seventy dollars.

The Regency was the epitome of luxury with its thick carpeted bedrooms and Italian marble and travertine tile bathrooms. A massive crystal chandelier hung above the black-and-white marble tiled lobby, decorated with antiques and French provincial furniture that set the standard in affluence. The far end of the hotel was comprised of several ballrooms and other large rooms that were available to rent for weddings and other events. Over the years as newer hotels opened, it lost its attraction and fell into a state of disrepair. When the owners filed for bankruptcy, it became an eyesore and a popular spot for vagrants to hide out.

It was slated for demolition until Jackson Devonshire, owner of Devonshire Enterprises, heard about the once glorious hotel. When he walked into the ramshackle building, he saw the true beauty of it. Other than the serious signs of neglect, the building could be salvaged. When he approached the city with an offer to buy it, it was immediately accepted.

Lexi applied for the job opening as soon as she saw it; this was her dream job. She would be partly responsible for helping preserve a piece of Louisiana history and restore an older building back to its glorious splendor.

It was a long time coming, but now when she looked at The Regency, she saw how it looked when it first opened its doors. It had been returned to its original splendor and sophistication and gone was the dilapidated historical monstrosity.

Tonight, a Mardi Gras ball was being held in one of the long forgotten ballrooms. Romantic string music from the orchestra filled the night air and complimented the delicate chimes of champagne flutes clinking.

Tonight's ball was the perfect opportunity for the high society of Springport, and surrounding towns, to see the beauty of the hotel with the completed renovations. It had been carefully gutted so that it could be restored. Lexi spent endless hours researching fixtures from that era in an attempt to replace any originals that were beyond repair. If the originals could not be replaced, she located similar ones. When she looked around at the final product, she knew the meticulous work had been worth it.

As she moved through the crowd, she smiled at the guests. The women wore extravagant gowns that probably cost more than her monthly salary, and the men were equally as handsome with their tailored tuxedos. So far, everything was a grand success. It appeared that Louisiana's elite had no problem relinquishing money to help restore their heritage. The tickets for the ball cost a small fortune, but no one seemed to mind the cost. As word about the ball spread to more people, curiosity about this once spectacular hotel being restored to its original grandeur, and not a seedy hotel, became the focus.

If only her husband, Bennett, could be here. Unfortunately, something had come up at work. But thankfully, Kyle had come. She smiled at her friend as he surveyed the crowd. She could not deny that he was a handsome man who attracted quite a few stares from women hoping to catch his eye.

His broad shoulders filled out the superb lines of the tuxedo he wore. He talked to those around him with an easy banter and a knockout smile. However, she knew that he would rather be any place other than here, especially since The Gazette ran an article about him being Louisiana's most eligible bachelor. Women called him at all times of the night, sent seductive emails, and slipped him phone numbers at the oddest places.

However, he ignored their advances. Somehow, he had remained single, even with the attention women threw his way.

Chapter 2

Lexi stared at the numbers creeping up on the gas pump in exasperation. Maybe she should have listened to Bennett before buying this car. She never did like to show off or draw attention toward herself, but as soon as she saw this car, she had to have it. With her recent promotion and raise, she could easily afford a car note. It took her a while to convince Bennett. He was against purchasing another car, wanting to use the extra money for vacations and anything else they may wish to splurge on. However, she knew that he would spend the extra money on items for himself without bothering to consult her. For once, she wanted to spend the money on herself. It was her money after all; money that she worked hard to earn.

Lately, Lexi had prided herself on being a hard-working and sensible woman. One who was organized, planned ahead and made good choices.

But a part of her had missed resilient, feisty, and courageous woman she had been as a young adult.
For some unknown reason, Lexi saw this car as a way to relive her youth.

Now if only the weather was friendlier more than a few days out of the year, she could enjoy her Infiniti G37 hardtop convertible. She loved riding around town with the top down, but the weather had been far from cooperative with her lately.

She should have listened to her gut instinct and flown instead of driving from Springport, Louisiana to Winston-Salem, North Carolina. Her boss had recently purchased another dilapidated hotel, and he wanted her to help with the renovations. It would have been faster to fly, but in all of her infinite wisdom, she thought she would be able to make a few stops along the way and check out several antique stores. Except, she never had a chance to stop at even one store.

While she waited for the gas tank to fill she tried to call her husband again and groaned as her call went unanswered. She sent him a quick text, informing him that she would be home soon.

Lately, she could not seem to do anything right when it came to what he wanted. He found fault with everything she did. Well, she had news for him; he was no picnic to live with either. He was notorious for leaving his dirty clothes and shoes all over the house, and he never flushed the toilet. But tolerating another person's habits was all part of marriage. She wished he would stop dwelling on her shortcomings and accept her for who she was. Instead, he made her life miserable with his constant complaining.

At times, her heart ached for the love they shared for each other in the beginning. When she first met

Bennett, he was not only handsome, but also charismatic and determined. That very charisma and determination was what attracted her to him. He was the man of her dreams. She had finally met her Prince Charming.

In the beginning, they could not keep their hands off each other and spent all of their free time together. Only, these last three years their time together had dwindled down. Now they rarely even ate their meals together. Some days they went without saying more than five words to each other.

She had the fancy white wedding along with her perfect groom. Standing over six feet tall, he had broad shoulders, dark wavy hair, and mesmerizing eyes. He was, and still is, a heartthrob. Even now, when she looked at him, her heart raced.

The recent lack of communication and intimacy saddened her. Sometimes she wished she could turn back time. If she had done something different, would their marriage have been better? Maybe if she had spent more time focusing on him instead of her career, her marriage would not be as strained as it was. Doubt constantly showed its ugly head lately. There were so many "what if" questions.

As the gas pump finally hit full, she waited for the receipt to print out so that she could place it in the envelope she kept in the car. While waiting, she went through the junk Bennett had stuffed in the console when he borrowed the car two weeks ago. As usual, he promised to clean everything up; yet, the center console had remained cluttered. Honestly, how hard was it to either place the receipt in the envelope she had for just that reason or throw the blasted piece of paper away? She swore he did this to aggravate her. He complained that she was too compulsive and orderly in the way she wanted things organized.

At the bottom of the console, she found a crumpled receipt. As she straightened it out, her heart caught in her throat. On top, as clear as day, was the name "Springport Inn". Why would a receipt for Springport Inn be in her car? It was one of the sleazy motels in town; one that allowed guests to pay by the hour. And, as far as she knew, there was no bar in the small hotel.

Confused, she looked at the paper again and confirmed that it was for the Springport Inn, and her husband had signed it!

For the rest of the drive home, her mind felt oddly disconnected from her body. The weather matched her mood as storm clouds moved in and a light mist fell. The road in front of her was a shiny black ribbon stretching out in front of her for miles. She gripped the steering wheel tightly as panic welled up inside of her. Rage quickly replaced the panic.

Was he having an affair? Was this why he regularly took cash withdrawals from their checking account? Unable to help herself, she skimmed over the receipt again and reconfirmed that it was her husband's signature at the bottom. Dropping it on the passenger seat, she clutched the steering wheel as her gut churned.

She kept telling herself this had to be a mistake; that he would not have an affair. As reality set in, a barrage of emotions attacked her. Anger, disgust, and sadness all struck her breaking heart at the thought of him betraying her in such a way. Did their marriage mean so little to him that he would seek out another woman? Did she mean so little to him?

Married for five years, she recently began to fear that their marriage was not as perfect as she wanted to believe. She realized that marrying the man of her dreams did not mean that her life would be a fairytale. When she said "I do" though, she thought that meant they would grow old together.

Now, she suspected her husband of infidelity. What made it worse was that he did it at one of the sleaziest hotels in town. Unanswered questions plagued her mind; how long had this been going on behind her back? Did he screw his mistress and then come home to make love to her? Did he use protection or did he infect her with some sexually transmitted disease?

Was this a mistress or, worse, a woman he picked up for a quickie?

They had to discuss this; she needed to know the truth. Once she got home, he would answer her questions. She refused to stay with a man who cheated on her. If true, their marriage was finished.

When she pulled up to the house, she was relieved to find him at home. At least he made an effort to welcome her back. As she walked up to the house, she felt as if she was outside of her body. Her heart pounded hard in her chest as she unlocked the door.

When he greeted her at the door with open arms, she wondered if his smile was for her or for memories of what he did while she was away. "I missed you."

For a moment she was speechless. She found it difficult to keep the anger from registering in her voice, "I just bet you have."

His smile wavered as he picked up on the tone in her voice. She flashed the hotel receipt in front of his face. He looked at her confused as the silence between the two of them grew thick. With a cold glare, she spat out, "I found this in the car today."

Stammering for a moment, he explained, "I...I planned on telling you tonight. I've been seeing April Hanson."

The ground beneath her opened up as her whole world came crashing down around her. She swallowed back a sob as a single tear raced down her cheek. *How could Bennett do this to me? How could I have been so gullible, so foolish, so stupid?* She licked her lips, garnering the courage to speak, the wisdom to know exactly what to say, and not allow her anger to take over. "Well..." She began, swallowing, "how long has this been going on?"

"Several months now."

As she fought back the tears, she watched his face for some flicker of remorse, but there was only a tightness in his face. "Was she the only one?"

He held up a hand, as if to stop her from coming near him. "I swear she is the only one. It just happened. We fell in love at first sight." Looking Lexi in the eyes, "I want a divorce."

His last statement sent daggers straight to her heart. She thought he loved her. Had her entire marriage been a complete farce? "I don't understand. How could you do this to me?"

"Seriously, Lexi, not everything is about you. I told you, it just happened. It's not as if I was looking around." Bennett let out an irritated sigh and ran his hand through his hair. "Look, Lexi, we both know that our marriage has been stale for some time. It is over. End of story. We are done, and I want out."

Her cheeks burned and her insides felt as if they had turned to ice.

He was dismissing their marriage as if it was a minor indiscretion in his life. His words hurt her more than imaginable.

Looking into Bennett's eyes, Lexi realized their marriage had meant nothing at all to him, and neither did she.

Without saying another word, she walked up the stairs to their bedroom and straight into the closet. She began throwing his clothes into one big pile.

"What are you doing?" he asked. His annoyance with her was obvious.

His betrayal had her life crumbling down around her, and she wanted to hurt him as bad as he hurt her. She replied angrily. "Helping you pack!"

Without waiting for him to answer, she opened the window and grabbed a large armful of clothes from the heap. She threw the clothes out the window and watched as they fluttered to the ground.

Astonished at her behavior, "Have you lost your mind?"

"You said you wanted to leave, so I am helping you pack." She told him in a sarcastic tone.

Before she could throw any more of his clothes out the window, he started grabbing the clothes she piled up on the floor. As he raced to pick up his clothes, she opened his dresser drawers, walked to the window, and emptied the contents outside.

His brow furrowed in anger, "Lexi, you need to stop this craziness. You are being childish. Let's handle this like adults."

She ignored his pleas for her to stop and proceeded to throw his belongings out the window. By now, the neighbors had gathered outside, curious to find out what was happening. A gust of wind moved through the yard and articles of his clothing fluttered about gaily.

As he rushed down the stairs and outside to pick up his clothes, she laughed at his antics. She chuckled to herself, "Serves him right."

He yelled angrily up to the open window, and shook a fist at her, "You are insane! This is really immature Lexi."

Hurt caused by his indiscretions exploded inside of her as she yelled, "How dare you call me immature! You are the one banging another woman!"

Next, she tossed out his keys and wallet. Before he had a chance to react, she slammed the window shut. After running downstairs, locking the doors, and making sure the chains were also engaged, she slumped onto the couch. She let her face fall into her hands as the tears rolled down her cheeks.

How could she be so stupid? How did she miss the signs that he was cheating on her? The sound of Bennett pounding on the door interrupted her thoughts. "Go away, Bennett."

"Come on Lexi, don't be like this. Let's talk about this like adults."

In a dismissive tone, she quipped, "There is nothing to talk about. I am sure that your mistress will let you spend the night at her house."

She stared bleakly at the floor. Various emotions assaulted her mind, as the old saying once a cheater, always a cheater kept playing in her mind like a broken record. She would not give him a chance to cheat on her again; she had too much pride and self-respect to do that.

She never once found their lovemaking lacking. Yet now, he was telling her he found someone he actually loved. What did that say about their relationship? What did she mean to him?

As she tried to wrap her mind around everything that happened today, she filtered out the incessant pounding on the door. It did not matter how hard he knocked; she refused to open the door. She would not allow him back in, not while she still lived here.

She closed her ears to the cajoling whine of his voice as he called her various vile, degrading names. Now who was being immature? She closed her eyes in hopes of blocking out the sounds around her.

As his footsteps receded from the house, she waited to hear his car start. As it peeled away from the curb, she pulled an afghan tight over her body. This was such a blow to her. She was not sure which path she wanted to take, but she could not live here. She would always wonder if he brought his mistress to this very house and into their marriage bed when she was out of town. No, it would be best to break it off altogether. She needed to start her life with a clean slate with nothing around her that reminded her of him and his betrayal. She walked upstairs to the bedroom and stuffed what belongings she could into a suitcase. For now, she would stay at The Regency.

She felt so destroyed. How could she not know he was seeing someone else?

Despair and heartache welled up inside of her. She could barely breathe, barely think. Silent tears rolled from her eyes as she thought about the last few years of her marriage.

When people talked about love, they spoke about the positive emotions. The butterflies they felt in their stomach, the desire they had for each other, and the happiness associated with love. No one talked about how it felt when your love was betrayed. No one talked about how it felt to have your heart ripped out of you. No one mentioned how difficult it would be to continue living as you immersed yourself in darkness.

- - - - - - ● - - - - - - - - -

Lexi groaned when the phone rang. She kept telling herself that it would not be her mother, but when she saw the caller ID she knew it was. Something deep inside of her told her that somehow her mom knew what had transpired earlier. Either one of her neighbors called her mom, or Bennett had. Lexi answered her phone with a strained voice, "Hi, Mom."

"Honey, what's wrong?"

Lexi rubbed her temples. This was going to be a hard conversation. "I don't want to talk about it right now mom. Can it wait?"

"I am sick with worry. I heard that you and Bennett had a fight and that you threw his clothes out the window."

*Well, it did not take long for someone to go running to her mothe*r. Lexi thought to herself. "Mom, I just can't talk about it right now. I need time to think."

"I'm coming over."

In a rushed tone, "No, that isn't necessary. I will tell you everything later. I promise, I am fine."

"Well, I will let you get some rest for now. But I want to know what is going on. I'm sure the whole town is talking about your little dramatic act."

Of course, her mom would see it as a dramatic act when Lexi felt as if her world was coming to an end, and her mom was more concerned about what other people thought.

Chapter 3

It amazed her how your life could change in the blink of an eye. She had been so upset over everything that happened with Bennett, it was not until this morning she realized her period was MIA – missing in action. That one realization shook her very being. She could not help but worry, even if it might be over nothing. She had never been regular and with the added stress of her current situation, of course her period would be late. Still, she was over two weeks late. But she could not be pregnant, she had been on the pill for years now.

She paced the bathroom floor as she waited. Deep down, she knew what the stick would say, but she prayed it would not. It was not as if she had any control over this matter, what was done was done.

As she waited, she re-read the directions on the back of the box to make sure that she'd read them correctly.

> *Take any time. Results in three minutes. 99% accuracy.*

When she went to the pharmacy last night, all the tests looked idiot proof. Just pee on a stick and you get the results in three minutes.

As if knowing that she could not stand to wait another second, her timer went off. Biting her bottom lip, she slowly turned toward the test. When she saw the results, tears came to her eyes. She was pregnant.

She dropped to the floor of the bathroom. A baby! A flurry of emotions ran through her as her heart beat rapidly at just the thought of a baby. She was about to embark upon a phase in her life that she had not considered in a long time---*Motherhood.*

Leaning against the wall, she tapped the pregnancy test against the floor. Chewing on her bottom lip, her thoughts moved to a tiny human being growing inside of her.

During this past year, her life had changed drastically, and now, she was pregnant. She had to tell Bennett, but, right now, she could not even gather enough courage to talk to him. Besides, she could not stand the thought of being in the same room with him, much less telling him that they were expecting a baby.

She was also afraid to tell him. He had always been adamant that he did not want children. Yet, here she was pregnant with no husband. This was NOT how she pictured her life.

During her lunch hour, she ran over to the local bookstore in search of a pregnancy book. She wanted one that provided a week by week breakdown of what to expect. She was curious about the changes her body was going through, and the baby's development. Plus, she needed pointers on what she should be doing. Now was not the time to ask her mother for advice.

When she walked into the bookstore, she inhaled deeply. She found the smell of a bookstore intoxicating. While she could have downloaded a book on her eBook reader, there was something to be said about holding a book in your hands. Plus, she wanted something she could tab, highlight, and mark how she saw fit.

As she perused the shelves of books, she wished she had more time to spend in the store. She had been so busy lately that she had not taken the time to do things she enjoyed.

When she found the shelves housing the pregnancy books, she was taken aback by the sheer volume of books out there on the subject. She assumed there would be a few books, but this was more than she expected. How in the world was she supposed to choose the best book?

Chapter 4

Lexi kept reminding herself that today was a new day. She was beginning a new phase in her life. She still found it hard to believe that she had been separated from Bennett for five weeks now. While she did not regret her decision, she did miss waking up to a warm body beside her and the companionship. Although, truth be told, this last year they spent more time away from each other than together.

That morning, breakfast did not go easily for Lexi. Eyeing the eggs suspiciously, she breathed deeply to keep her stomach from doing somersaults. Even after she managed to hold down some dry toast, her stomach remained queasy.

Nausea rolled through her, tightening her stomach and making her mouth water. Her stomach rolled again. She swallowed and leaned forward.

One hand raised to her mouth, she raced to the bathroom. For long moments afterward, she remained on the floor, her knees weak and a sour taste in her mouth.

Perhaps a run would help settle her stomach and emotions. As she took her morning run, she was so deep in thought that she did not even notice the morning sun as it rose over the treetops. She picked up speed, breaking into a jog as she reached The Magnolia Inn, Mr. Devonshire's newest hotel.

It was time for her to stop hiding out in North Carolina. When Mr. Devonshire had asked her three weeks ago to oversee the final renovations of The Magnolia Inn, she had quickly accepted. She saw it as the perfect opportunity to run away from her problems, but it was time to return to Springport. When she returned home, she would start searching for a house to rent. While she was ready to begin her new life, she was not prepared to buy another home. Besides, until the divorce was finalized, she and Bennett still had a mortgage on the house they had shared. He could have the house, but she wanted her name removed from the paperwork. Let him figure out how to refinance the house in this market. It was not her problem anymore.

Now, to figure out what to do with her life. She was no longer the woman who had married Bennett, she had changed. She would never be that woman again, and that was okay. Her world would not come to an end because Bennett taught her how untrustworthy men were.

As a teenager, Lexi had been effervescent, outgoing, and quirky. Over the years she matured and lost her sense of individuality. Bennett had shattered her self-esteem. It was time for her to find that optimistic teenager from her past. The carefree spirit she had back then.

However, if she wanted to move on, she had to stop dwelling on the past. Instead, she needed to focus on what the future held. Instead of trying to alter an irreversible reality, she needed to move on with her life. She needed to accept what happened and continue on with life in spite of it.

- - - - - - ●● ● ●● - - - - - -

After her run, she jumped in the shower. As she combed her hair, she realized that she had kept the same hairstyle since she married Bennett. Pinning her auburn hair up in a loose bun, she decided it was time for a change and called Henri to cut her hair. She had met Henri last week at a coffee shop a block from the hotel. He gave her a business card and begged her to let him cut her hair. At the time, just the thought of another change in her life scared her.

Looking at her reflection in the mirror, she noticed that even her brown eyes had lost their sparkle, making the dark circles under her eyes visible. She dabbed concealer around them before applying the rest of her makeup.

She walked over to the closet and chose a simple business suit and sensible shoes. As she checked her watch, she groaned. She would be late for her meeting with Mr. Devonshire if she did not hurry.

She had not told anyone about her pregnancy, but she would have to tell her boss soon. She prayed this did not affect her job. With the new projects they were working on, the pregnancy may make it difficult to travel. If it meant that she had to drive to each location, then so be it.

That was one conversation she was not looking forward to either. The promotion was still fairly recent, and she feared that he might pull her new position. Then what would she do?

She hoped that being good at her job would be her saving grace. She had the managerial skills needed to help this company grow. Mr. Devonshire had been so impressed with the work that she had done in restoring The Regency, that he asked her to take over as the manager. She loved her job and had always enjoyed working with people. In her current position, she had a chance to work with an assortment of people. Unlike other hotel managers, she preferred to listen to the comments that customers had and used their recommendations to help make the hotel a better place to stay.

This job was what kept her going after she and Bennett separated, well, that and the baby. As she was walking downstairs to the lobby, her cell phone rang. She let out a groan when she saw that it was her brother, “Good morning, Jason.”

"Lexi, I wanted to make sure that you will be home this weekend. I have everything arranged for our parent's anniversary party."

The last thing she wanted was to celebrate a wedding anniversary. "I am wrapping everything up here so that I can be home for the weekend."

"Look, Lexi, I know that you are dragging out your stay in North Carolina so you don't have to see Bennett. But you need to snap out of it."

The harshness in Jason's voice rattled her nerves. He had no idea what she was going through. Heck, he had it all, the perfect family and an amazing job. She was not ready to forgive Bennett for his betrayal, and she would appreciate some support from her family. Was that too much to ask?

It was too soon for her to forgive Bennett; the heartache still too blinding. She had hoped that coming to North Carolina to work for a while would help ease the pain, but even here everything reminded her of Bennett. If only she could erase him from her mind and out of her life. But the life she carried inside of her would be a constant reminder of him.

"It will break our parents' hearts if you aren't there Lexi."

Guilt washed over her as Jason played this card. It was unfair, but he knew that she would do whatever was in her power to keep from disappointing her parents.

As guilt settled deep in the pit of her stomach, she promised to show up for their parents' party, where she would most likely be talked about behind her back. The thought of everyone staring at her was not particularly welcoming.

As she hung up the phone, she realized that her and Bennett's wedding anniversary was also coming up. She felt like such a failure as a wife. Maybe if she had tried to be a better wife, he would not have sought the arms of another woman.

It was time for her to do some soul-searching and make some life-changing decisions. Perhaps she should consider moving to North Carolina and starting a new life, but that would mean Bennett won. She refused to let him force her to move away from her family, even if they did tend to drive her crazy. Besides, if she moved away, her child would not grow up near either of the grandparents, and she did not want that. No matter how many times her mom rattled her nerves, she meant well, and she would spoil her grandchild rotten.

Taking the afternoon off, Lexi went shopping before she went to the beauty salon. She could not believe that she was doing this. Had she lost her mind? She always planned everything out and never did anything on impulse. Kyle and Bennett picked on her about her being the level-headed one among them. Yet, here she was, doing something completely out of character. When she called Henri, and he told her to come this afternoon, she did not want to give herself a chance to back out. And as she looked down at her new outfit, she realized that it was time to move forward.

Ever since she found out that she was pregnant, she started looking at her life in a different way. She still wondered how Bennett could do this to her, and with someone like April Hanson? That woman reminded her of a Barbie doll except with an enormous pair of tatas that would give her back problems in a few years, if not already. April was everything that Lexi wasn't. April was a carefree spirit with no worries in life, with legs that went on for miles, long blond hair, and the bluest eyes that had to be manufactured by a pair of contacts. Her tan was probably fake, as well.

Walking into the door of the beauty salon, Lexi took a deep breath. *Well, here's to the start of my new life.*

As she walked over to the hairdresser's station, Henri was shaking his head at her. "Girl, I can't believe that you are going to let me get at that hair. I have wanted to give your hair some new life since we first met."

She laughed at Henri as she kissed him on each cheek, "Well, if I am getting ready to start a new life, I may as well do it right."

Henri tsked as he walked around her, "Well, I want you to look like the hot woman that you are. I know women who pay thousands of dollars for a figure like yours and would kill for the color of your hair. You can't get that color from a bottle." Patting the chair, he told her, "Now, have a seat so that I can give you a style worthy of your beauty."

She could not bring herself to look in the mirror until he finished, so she nervously waited.

After he had finished, Henri spun her around in the swivel chair, lifted her chin, and pointed to the mirror, "Voila! Now, look at yourself, love."

She gasped at the image in the mirror. Henri had transformed her. He added long layers with bangs that just brushed her eyebrows. The haircut was feminine yet still sophisticated. It gave her a look of confidence, especially in the black pencil skirt, sapphire blue silk top and black knee-high boots with two-inch heels she had purchased earlier. She could not remember the last time she looked, and felt, this good.

She was so stunned at how great the hairstyle looked on her, she could not find the words to tell him thank you.

Chapter 5

Huge raindrops fell from the night sky and pelted against the windshield of Lexi's car. She watched through fatigued eyes as the wipers slapped them away. The swooshing noise of the wipers lured her toward the complete exhaustion that she'd fought for the last half hour. When she felt herself drifting off to sleep, she opened the window.

She had been working non-stop in an attempt to forget about Bennett. A short day for her was putting in twelve hours. Her usual work day entailed sixteen plus hours, but now she had a feeling that she would have to take it a lot easier.

As if on cue, her phone rang, "Hey, Mom."

"Hey, honey. How are you doing?"

Holding back a sigh, she replied, "I am doing okay. I am on my way home. I should be at The Regency later on tonight."

"You know that you are always welcome to stay at the house."

"I appreciate the offer Mom, but I have a few things to catch up on at the office before taking off for the weekend."

"If you say so."

Lexi shook her head as she hung up the phone. Her mom meant well, but if she stayed at her parents' house her mom would see it as the perfect opportunity to try and convince Lexi to drop the divorce proceedings and stop this "foolishness".

As soon as she arrived at The Regency, she walked straight over to her office. She dropped her purse and luggage near the door and walked over to her desk. She picked up the mail stacked high in her mail basket and flipped through it. Most of it was the usual business stuff and could wait until Monday.

She had hoped something pressing had come up that would keep her detained. Anything to prevent her from attending the party since her rat of a husband would be there. She could strangle Jason for even inviting him. It was as if he did not care about her feelings.

- - - - - - - ● ● ● ● ● - - - - - - - -

When Lexi drove up to her parents' house, she dug deep into her inner self to find the strength to handle today. Disgust moved through her when she saw that Bennett was already there. Forcing a smile on her face, she walked up to the front door.

Before she could knock, her mother opened the door. She whispered, "Be nice, you hear me."

She wrinkled her nose and nodded her head with a little too much enthusiasm. "Mom, of course I will be nice. After all, I don't want to be the one who ruined your anniversary party."

Her mother kissed her on the cheek and walked inside with her. As Lexi looked around, she had to begrudgingly admit that Jason had done a fantastic job with setting up the party. But, then why would he not, he had a great wife to lean on.

Lexi was pouring herself a cup of coffee when her Aunt Mitzi came to stand beside her.

"Your dad mentioned to Uncle Scott and I that you and Bennett were splitting up. How come?"

Lexi gave her a smirk, "We just fell out of love. Our marriage had run its course."

She raised her eyebrows, "Was he fooling around on you?"

Lexi gave her a bewildered look, "No..."

"Oh, I bet he was. He has that look about him." She gave Lexi a grin, "Want me to put a hex on him?" She asked.

Lexi chuckled, "As nice as that sounds, I'm sure it would backfire on me. I think I'll let him be some other poor woman's problem."

Her Aunt Mitzi looked disappointed, "You know, in the old days, women had a remedy for cheating men."

Curiosity got the better of Lexi, "What kind of remedy?"

"A wife would put the voodoo on her cheating man so that he couldn't come to attention." Her Aunt Mitzi leaned in towards Lexi, "And if I were you, I would consider putting the voodoo on him for sure. I can get you something to put in his coffee."

As her Aunt Mitzi walked away, Lexi laughed as she shook her head. As nice as putting a hex on Bennett sounded, knowing her luck, it would backfire.

- - - - - - - - - ● - - - - - - - - - -

Her mother's lips were set into a taut, pained shape as she looked over at Lexi with a disapproving stare. This was supposed to be a celebration and, yet, her mother was preparing to lecture her. Her mother may not have said it in so many words, but her facial expressions said it all. She had had this fixed expression on her face ever since Lexi told her about the divorce.

She used her fork to push the cake around the plate, but she could not bring herself to devour it. Worse, the cake was her favorite, white almond cake with a decadent buttercream frosting with a hint of almond and a tangy pineapple filling. Between the pregnancy and her mom's attitude, she could not enjoy the dessert.

Her mother could be very opinionated, but today, she was pressing the issue too much for Lexi. "I'm disappointed in the way you avoided Bennett while he was here for the party Lexi."

Lexi gripped her fork so tight, her knuckles turned white. "Mom, did you honestly expect me to welcome him with open arms?"

"Lexi, honey, he is still part of this family, and you should have at least acknowledged that he was here. I don't think you have actually stopped to think about your decision?"

She forced herself not to roll her eyes and bit her lip to keep from saying anything. When she saw Bennett, it took all of her willpower not to cause a scene. Instead, she busied herself in the kitchen. Now, her mom acted like Lexi was in the wrong. "Mom, I have thought long and hard about this. I refuse to stay with a man who no longer loves me."

Her mom had never been shy about expressing her emotions - even overshared at times. This happened to be one of those times. "I wish you would think this through. You are making the biggest mistake of your life. It breaks my heart to see the two of you separated."

She took a deep, calming breath as she faced her mom, trying not to show how shaken she was by her mother's words. She expected opposition from her mother, but nothing to this degree. "My mind is made up, Mom. I'm not changing it."

Her mom shook her head, her blond bob swinging sharply with the movement. "You shouldn't throw away all those years of marriage on one tiny indiscretion. Perhaps if you gave it more time? It takes a lot of work to make a marriage succeed. I know he hurt you, but that doesn't mean he couldn't, or shouldn't, be forgiven."

Letting out an exasperated sigh, she bit back the retort on the tip of her tongue. No one knew more than her just how hard she had to work at her marriage, but she refused to stay with a husband who could not remain faithful. "Mom, he doesn't love me. No amount of work will change the way he feels about me. He is in love with someone else."

"Well, maybe if you had devoted time to your husband instead of your job, he wouldn't have found another woman to love."

Gritting her teeth, she warned, "Mom, seriously that is enough."

Instead of making another statement, her mother surveyed her with eyes that perceived far more than they should. She loved her mother to death, but she refused to believe that her daughter was doing the right thing by divorcing Bennett. In her mother's eyes, she should grin and bear whatever little indiscretions Bennett committed. After all, men would be men.

"You seemed to be so in love. I thought you had found your soul mate, honey."

Lexi blinked back the tears threatening to form, "And you think I didn't believe that as well? When we married, I thought we had the perfect life in our future. I loved him with all my heart." Her soon to be ex-husband's betrayal had taken an enormous chunk from her soul along with her heart.

"You are more than welcome to move back here. You are seldom home as it is."

Shaking her head, she stated, "I appreciate the offer, but I am going to live at the hotel for a while. Bennett is keeping the house, and I am looking for a house to rent."

"It's just that it has been so long since you lived here, and it would be nice spending time catching up on things."

Lexi found herself lost for words. She walked over and hugged her mom, "I will always need you, Mom. I just need some time for myself."

"Your father and I are always here for you."

"I know that you are, Mom."

- - - - - - - ● ● ● ● ● ● ● ● ● ● ● ● - - - -

Lexi walked outside, needing a minute to herself. Her mother's constant criticisms were beginning to wear on her.

Lexi's dad stepped outside and sat next to her on the glider. He patted her leg as Lexi turned to him and asked, "Dad, why is Mom the way she is? Why can't she accept me for being me?"

He pulled Lexi closer to him and told her, "Your mom is a complicated woman. She does not do well with change and when you announced that you and Bennett were divorcing, it took her out of her comfort zone. While she has never believed in divorce, I think it is fear of the unknown that upsets her more."

"So, she would rather I accept his infidelity and ignore his betrayal instead of moving on with my life." Lexi shook her head, "I don't think I could live my life being miserable."

Her dad sighed, "You have to remember that we come from a time when it was believed that problems in the marriage should be worked out. The Catholic religion always stressed that divorce is a sin."

"But so is adultery," Lexi conjectured.

"True. And I think that if that same thing were to happen to your mom, she would accept the affair - but she would make my life a living nightmare."

Lexi thought about what her dad said and burst into laughter, "I can see mom nagging you twenty-four/seven."

He scoffed, "Nagging? Nagging? She would do worse than nagging. She would badger me non-stop. I would not get a moments peace."

Lexi looked at her dad, "Do you think I should have stayed with Bennett?"

"Since you asked, I think Bennett got off easy. Had it been me, I would have tortured him before throwing him out on the street."

A weary smile tugged at her lips, "I considered it, but I was so hurt that the sight of him infuriated me."

Her dad kissed the top of her head, "Well, don't you worry about it. Something tells me Bennett will get his just desserts soon enough."

As they sat there watching the starry night, Lexi pondered what her dad had said. Had he done something to Bennett while he was here? Her dad had been awfully friendly to Bennett today and Lexi would not put it past her dad to do something. He had a silent way of getting even.

As Lexi sat in the hotel parking garage, she thought about how much of a disappointment she must be to her mother. Her mother did not believe in divorce, and her own daughter was doing the very thing she despised.

Walking towards the elevator, her vision blurred. As her hand reached out to grip onto something solid, she instantly regretted not eating anything today, but she had been too upset at the party to do so. Instead, she had just played with her food. As her brain whirled and her body trembled, she reminded herself that she had another little person to care for and skipping meals was no way to treat her ever-growing body.

Suddenly, the dizziness made it impossible to function. A voice sounded somewhere in the distance, "Lexi!" That baritone voice sounded familiar as it filtered through her foggy brain.

Shaking her head, she tried to clear the fuzziness enveloping her. She willed herself not to pass out on the cold concrete as her body swayed precariously.

As she started to fall, strong arms gripped her body, "Woman, you almost gave me a heart attack." The voice broke through the haziness in her mind as he lifted her to his rock hard chest.

She sighed in contentment and whispered, "Kyle."

His warmth was a comfort to her as she tried to focus in on her surroundings. She rested her spinning head against a broad, solid chest and was grateful that he was here. He asked, "Are you still staying at the hotel?"

She nodded her head, "Room 522." As the elevator moved, her stomach churned as her head continued to spin. As he stepped out of the elevator, he took the key she had in her purse and opened the door. Gently, he lowered her onto the bed and covered her with a blanket. While taking off her shoes, he asked, "Have you eaten today?"

Struggling to sit up, she shook her head.

Pushing her back down on the bed, he told her, "You stay lying down. I will run across the street and get you something to eat." As he headed for the door, he ordered her, "I don't want you to move one inch, you hear me?"

Too weak to answer, she curled up in the bed. "I just need something to eat is all."

"You look like death warmed over. You need to lay there and let me take care of you. What were you thinking by not eating today?"

No sooner than she closed her eyes, the smell of food woke her. Her stomach let out a loud rumble, reminding her again that she had not eaten.

With a concerned look, he handed her a plate of food, "I want you to eat and then you, young lady, need some rest."

The smell in the air caused her mouth to water, "Oh, my goodness, this smells heavenly."

"I hope you like it. All they had readily available was shrimp Alfredo with a slice of French bread."

Taking a bite of the warm pasta, she moaned in appreciation, "This is perfect. You should know by now that I love pasta."

After eating, her eyes drooped as fatigue consumed her. As Kyle moved the plates away, she snuggled under the comforter on the bed. Sighing, she closed her eyes just for a moment and, instead, fell into a deep slumber.

- - - - - - - - - - - - - - - - - -

Kyle watched Lexi as she slept. Since her separation with Bennett, she was more subdued than usual, but tonight she seemed even more dispirited.

Chapter 6

Kyle and Lexi met for their morning coffee before she headed off to work. As soon as she caught sight of him, her heart skipped a beat. Lately, she was seeing him as a man and not just a friend, which was dangerous territory. His friendship meant too much to her for her to become romantically involved with him; besides, she was still reeling from Bennett's betrayal.

But still, she could not deny that the man sitting across from her was sexy, and it had nothing to do with the expensive clothes he wore.

Kyle had the kind of arresting face you saw in a men's fashion magazine. He had it all; the brooding good looks, chiseled jaw, and bedroom eyes. He also exuded an animalistic power, and she would dread going head to head with him in a business meeting. A lethal beast hid right under the surface, waiting for the perfect moment to strike.

Every woman in the café wanted to be in her shoes right now. This man was the answer to their wildest dreams, hottest fantasies, and hearts' desires.

Kyle smiled over at her and said, "I wish we could spend more time together. We keep missing each other lately."

In a sarcastic tone, she jokingly stated, "Well, it's not like I can just walk away from my job. Unlike one of us in the room, I didn't sell my software company for fifty million dollars, and that doesn't count the money made before the sale."

"I still can't believe they made the purchase price public. It was supposed to be confidential. Somehow the overpriced lawyer missed that," he stated with a hint of annoyance.

"Even if they had kept it confidential, The Gazette would have pried it out of someone. After all, they consider you Louisiana's most eligible bachelor," she informed him matter of factly.

Shaking his head, he scoffed, "I can't believe they published that article. Ever since that article ran, I am swamped with calls and emails. I had to change my telephone numbers and cancel my social media accounts."

"Oh, you poor thing. I still don't understand why someone with your degrees and money wants to start a fishing charter business."

He shrugged his shoulders, "What else am I going to do?"

"I don't know - travel, enjoy your life."

"Vacations are overrated."

"Speak for yourself. I don't remember the last time I had a vacation." She looked at her watch. "And now, I'm going to be late. I can't afford to push my luck by being late."

Standing up, a wave of nausea hit, and her face became pasty white. He looked at her with concern on his face. "What's wrong? You look like a ghost. Are you okay?"

She took several deep breaths, trying to keep her coffee down. "I'm okay. My doctor told me that this part usually lasts for the first twelve weeks or so."

She could make out the smile on her friend's face. "That's wonderful. How far along are you?"

"Eight weeks, give or take."

"What does Bennett think about the news?"

With the nausea subsiding, she confessed, "I haven't told him yet. We still aren't speaking."

"I'm so sorry. I knew that you hadn't moved back in the house, but I wasn't sure if you guys were going to try and salvage your marriage. I don't want to pry, but have you tried counseling?"

"You are my best friend, so you aren't prying. I haven't talked about him because it is still too painful."

"I'm sorry. When do you plan on telling him about the baby?"

"I'm not sure. I have to tell him, but I need to build up the nerve first. I doubt he will even acknowledge the child is his. And apparently, when I stopped listening to his constant whining, he found a much younger, more sympathetic ear to complain to. But let's not talk about Bennett anymore."

"What about your parents? Do they know?"

Shaking her head, she said, "No, I haven't told them either. I will, of course. It's just that I dread the conversation with my parents, especially my mom. She is already harping on how I should take Bennett back, and this will make the nagging worse."

Kyle took her hand in his, "It isn't your fault that Bennett cheated on you. You cannot blame yourself for his adultery."

She was still in shock from Bennett's betrayal and her pregnancy. How had her life suddenly taken this turn? Somehow, she would get through this. She looked at her watch and groaned, "I hate to leave but I really need to get to work."

"Let's go out to supper one night. Get your mind off of your problems."

"That sounds good. I'll call you later on this week, and we can set up a date."

- - - - - - ●●●●●● ●●●●● - - - -

Lexi was helping the front desk clerk handle a complaint when Marlene Daigle, her witch of a mother-in-law, stormed into the hotel, and her gaze landed on Lexi. Lexi took an unconscious step backward as the outraged woman walked closer to her. "You!" She shouted, pointing an accusatory finger, "How dare you throw my son out of his own house!" The woman's face contorted in rage, "Now the whole town is talking about how Bennett's unmentionables were floating in the wind!"

"Well, if Bennett had remained faithful, none of this would've happened."

"Liar!" She screamed, "My Bennett would do no such thing. You have ruined his reputation in this town, you selfish little hussy."

Her face red with anger, she turned on her heels and went to leave as quickly as she had come. As her mother-in-law walked away, Lexi straightened her back, and called out, " Oh, Marlene, where are my manners? Would you like me to validate parking for your broom?"

She turned around and huffed, "My bro...ugh, well I never." Without uttering another word, she stormed out of the hotel.

As she left, Lexi let out a sigh of relief. All in all, it went better than Lexi thought it would have. Thinking back at what had transpired, perhaps Lexi should not have made the comment about the broom, but at the time it felt right. Besides, over the years her mother-in-law had gotten in plenty of rude digs on Lexi's behalf.

- - - - - - - - - - ● - - - - - - - - - - -

Kyle had always wondered how Lexi wound up marrying someone like Bennett Daigle. Bennett may be his friend, but he was one of those men entirely wrapped up in himself. If he had known that his best friend would be this cruel to her, he would have kicked his ass back then. Actually, kicking his ass did not seem like a bad idea right now. Maybe the man needed some sense knocked into him.

Kyle never told Lexi how people felt about her husband, even though she may have suspected. A part of him felt genuine remorse for the entire emotional trauma that she would endure because of the divorce. A larger part of him, most probably his selfish part, was glad about the prospect of her being single once again. He had been a fool for never letting her know he had feelings for her. He always kept them in check, not wanting to scare her away.

He had considered asking her out, but the fear of embarrassing himself kept him tongue-tied. He could not imagine anything more humiliating than letting his best friend know he had romantic feelings for her, especially if she did not feel the same way about him. It would crush him to find out that she saw him as a brother instead of a love interest.

Chapter 7

Lexi looked at Kyle with a smile on her face; she kissed his cheek affectionately. "Thanks for supper. I really needed it."

"It was my pleasure. I missed talking with you these last few years."

Lexi nodded. These last few years Bennett tried to keep the two friends apart, wanting to keep Kyle all to himself.

"You are too good of a friend, Kyle. You have let me whine and cry on your shoulder more than I should. I know that Bennett is your friend as well, and I shouldn't complain about him to you."

Kyle took her in his arms and gave her a warm hug, "I am always here for you. I disagree with the way Bennett acted."

On the drive home, Kyle could still feel the spot where Lexi had kissed him. It was warm to the touch as if she had branded him with her lips.

As he entered his house, he noticed how dark and unwelcoming it felt. It was as if Lexi's kiss stirred something deep inside of him tonight. During supper, his gaze kept drifting to her luscious body every chance he got.

Desire filled him tonight, desire for his best friend. As his brain tried to justify the urges he felt for her, he kept telling himself that it would never work. He did not want to risk his friendship with her. It meant too much to him.

Yet, he was only human and had noticed just how attractive she was. But even though he felt the pull of desire, it did not mean he had to act on it. He had met dozens of girls over the years, and he had always been able to control his actions.

An image of Lexi clouded his mind once more, this one of her glowing with a large belly. Soon she would give birth and his other best friend was the father of the child.

She was his best friend and always would be; yet, she was also so much more. She was feisty, intelligent and challenging. She had a good sense of humor and a good heart. Except now, he also saw her as one very desirable woman, who was suddenly very available.

She was not the kind of woman a man took lightly either, but she also kept her heart guarded. She may never want any man getting close to her. Just from talking to her, he knew that Bennett broke not only her heart, but also her trust in men. He had no idea how to mend her heart. For all he knew, if he did make a move, she would slap his face.

Chapter 8

Lexi decided today was the day she would go looking at apartments and houses. The first apartment reminded her more of a bachelor pad rather than a place to raise a family. However, it was a new development and the views were gorgeous.

The next was bright and airy. It had everything she wanted; it was near work and excellent school districts. It also had a huge balcony where she could entertain as she saw fit. The only thing preventing her from signing the papers was she could not see herself raising her child in an apartment.

She was about ready to give up when she saw an ad for an older house. She called and found out that the house was still available and, even better, that she could see it immediately.

When she drove up to the house, she knew it was meant for her. If she overlooked the overgrown yard and that the house needed a new paint job, she could see the hidden potential. A large weeping willow tree graced the front yard, and there was even a swing set in the back yard. It was as if the house was calling to her.

Her potential landlord was an elderly man. When he met her outside, he informed her, "I realize the house needs a lot of work. A lot of people have looked at the house and walked away. I had hoped to die in this house, but my daughter is determined to have me move in with her. I finally grew tired of her constant nagging and agreed. I can't bring myself to sell this house, so I decided to rent it instead. "

Once inside, she confirmed his statement about the house needing work. She told him, "Most of it appears to be purely cosmetic work."

Nodding his head, he explained, "My daughter's husband helps with any major repairs that come up. At my age, I don't see the point in painting. I have kept it the way my wife left the house before she passed away."

"The house is perfect. I can see myself bringing my child home from the hospital here."

Sadness filled his eyes for a moment as he reminisced, "My wife brought two children into this world here. Our son died serving his country in the Vietnam conflict." He picked up a picture from the wood mantle of the fireplace and handed it to her, "He was nineteen when he passed away. My wife lost her fight with cancer after that."

Lexi tenderly returned the picture back to its original place. As she looked around, she caught a glimpse of a future here in this house, a real future.

Kyle heard his phone ring and smiled when he saw it was Lexi calling, "What's up?"

He could tell she was excited about something by the way she quickly asked, "Are you busy?"

He let out a deep sigh, "I have been busy with the U.S. Coast Guard all day today. I didn't realize how much work went into starting a fishing charter company."

There was a hint of disappointment in her tone. "Well, I had wanted to meet for a cup of coffee, but that's okay. We can get together another night."

"Nonsense. I need to unwind after being cooped up all day." Plus, more than anything, he wanted to see her, if only for a little while.

When he made it to the café, the sky opened up. He rushed into the café to find Lexi already waiting for him. His breath caught as he looked at her; she looked positively gorgeous today with her auburn hair cascading down her back. Her eyes seemed to light up when she saw him.

His insides turned to jelly, and his tongue seemed to be stuck to the roof of his mouth. For the longest time, he envied Bennett. The body, the face, and the hair made her a sight to behold. As she reached up to hug him, her sensuous perfume captured his attention. "I hope you haven't been waiting long."

She shook her head, "No, not really. I was catching up on some emails while I waited." She looked outside, "If I had known that it would rain at any minute, I wouldn't have called."

"That's okay. It's just a little water."

At that moment, a loud boom of thunder rang out, rattling the windows of the café. She laughed, "Oh yeah, it's not raining hard."

As he listened to her talk, he still found it hard to believe that her marriage was over. It had taken a while for that fact to digest along with the fact that she was pregnant. And it infuriated him that Bennett was not stepping up to face the music.

He asked her, "So, do you want your usual, café au lait and beignets?"

Rubbing her belly, she replied, "I do, but this little one has me craving anything chocolate."

"Well, how about beignets filled with chocolate?"

Her mouth started watering at the thought and exclaimed, "Perfect."

- - - - - - - - - - ● - - - - - - - - - - -

As she watched Kyle, she had to admit that perhaps selling the business and working outside more agreed with him. His tanned, hard body did not come from strictly working out in the gym.

She was not sure if it was her pregnancy hormones or something else, but tonight he took her breath away. She always thought he looked handsome in his business suits, but there was something so down to earth about him dressing casually. She could get lost staring into his eyes; they were so penetrating, mesmerizing, and paralyzing all at the same time. When he first looked at her tonight, she felt desired, wanted, and appreciated. Lately, his banter had been more flirtatious and being with him tonight had her insides electrified.

As he walked over to their table, he was cautious not to spill anything on the tray he carried. He set down the tray and teased, "So, it sounds like this baby is going to have a sweet tooth."

Nodding her head, she replied, "I have to watch it, or I will gain more than just baby weight."

He looked up and down her body appreciatively, "I think you look gorgeous as usual."

As soon as he placed the plate in front of her, the sugary scent of hot beignets greeted her. When she bit into the warm fluffy pastry, the greasy sweetness filled her mouth as the chocolate rushed forward onto her tongue. They were soft as cotton and light as air; it was like biting into a heavenly pillow of doughnut goodness. Each bite melted in her mouth as it tantalized her taste buds. She let out a moan of pleasure as she devoured another one. How could something so good be so bad for you?

Kyle sipped his café au lait and a shiver of desire rushed through her. She needed to get a grip on her runaway hormones or she may try to pick up any man on the street.

As they sat drinking their coffee, his eyes penetrated her very soul once more. He seemed to be on the verge of saying something; the heat of his gaze hinted at his true feelings. If he felt the same way she did, they could melt the polar ice caps.

As she returned her drink to the table, he reached across and took her hand in his. His touch was tender, thoughtful, and full of emotion. His thumb rubbed across the top of her knuckles, heating her blood as goosebumps raced up and down her body.

Taking a deep breath, she asked, "So, how did your meeting go?"

"It went all right. I found a few boats to look at; one in Louisiana, but three are in Florida. I also put out a few feelers with staffing agencies to see if any fishing charter captains were looking for jobs. I assumed that it would be easy to buy a boat and hire someone to run it, but I was wrong. However, I refuse to give up on this dream."

"You shouldn't. If anything, I learned that life can change in the blink of an eye. You need to live it to the fullest."

"Even with this economy, there appears to be a steady demand for deep water fishing. If I can get the boat at the right price, I won't have to charge an arm and a leg for customers to fish."

"I have faith that you will do it."

"There are plenty of boat brokers out there with used boats for sale. I am also keeping a lookout for companies about to go under and need someone to buy their boats before the bank repossesses them."

She groaned, "I wish you could organize my life as well as you do yours. My personal life is a mess, and I keep putting everything off instead of tackling it."

Chapter 9

Lexi was excited to move everything of hers from the house she shared with Bennett and into her new home. It was time to start a few new chapters in her life, and one of those chapters began with the baby she was carrying.

As she pulled up to get the last of her items out of the house, she groaned when she saw April's car there. Just the thought of talking to the woman sent a shooting pain straight through her, directly to her heart. Little by little she had learned that almost everyone in town knew Bennett was fooling around during their marriage.

It was a slap in her face that he did not even wait for the divorce to be finalized before moving his tart into their house. And to make matters worse, he did not wait for Lexi to remove the rest of her items before doing so.

She tried to find a reason for Bennett acting the way he did. She thought maybe it could be a midlife crisis, but, heck, most men went out and bought a sports car for their midlife crisis. NOT have an affair. Perhaps Kyle was correct in his assumption that Bennett was jealous of her success and acted out. After all, her career was skyrocketing, and his career was plummeting.

All this time she would come home from her business trips, sporting sexy lingerie, giving him extra TLC, and he had been screwing another woman.

Before she could step out of her car to inform April that she needed the rest of her items, another car pulled up into the driveway. A tall, muscular man, who looked like he belonged in a bar, rather than in this neighborhood, got out. Even from her car, she could see the numerous tattoos that covered his body, including his bald head. The wife-beater T-shirt and faded blue jeans appeared to be painted on his body. Curiosity filled her as she watched the man make his way to the door. Hmm, had April already grown bored with Bennett and found herself another distraction? Just the thought of April cheating on Bennett cheered her up immensely. That very thought proved how much this nasty divorce had changed her. Before all of this, she had never wished ill of anyone, but now she could not wait for karma to give Bennett a taste of his own medicine.

She looked at her cell phone and tossed around the idea of calling Bennett and asking him to come let her in the house, so that he could see what his girlfriend was up to. She could already picture his face when he discovered April doing the nasty with another man.

As she watched the man ring the doorbell, she was amazed when April opened the door in an almost sheer nightie. Ugh, now she wished she had called

Bennett to the house.   Deciding not to wait for the lovebirds to finish whatever they had planned for the day, she started her car and drove away.

Chapter 10

Kyle reached over and slapped the alarm clock when it went off. He pulled the covers over his head, wanting a few extra minutes of sleep. He had tossed and turned most of the night because thoughts of Lexi clouded his mind.

He could not stop wondering what would happen when she told Bennett that she was pregnant. Would he want this child? Bennett never mentioned wanting to start a family, but then again, Bennett never confided in him that he was seeing someone else on the side.

Knowing that Lexi would soon be single again had stirred up emotions that he long ago buried. When she married Bennett, he assumed that he missed his chance with her. Now, he began to wonder if he did have a chance with Lexi.

The thought of her caused his heart to beat faster, so he tossed back the covers, made sure the alarm was turned off, and headed for the shower.

He reminded himself that he would not only be involved in a relationship with Lexi but that she was carrying Bennett's child.

Thinking of Bennett and how he wanted nothing to do with his child had anger sweltering inside of him. He should stand up and take responsibility.

He had to decide if he wanted to take on a relationship with Lexi but also care for another man's child. Could he raise another man's baby, a man he once considered to be a friend?

- - - - - - ● - ● - ● - - - - - -

After his meeting in town, Kyle headed over to the hotel. A smile formed on his face when he saw her standing in the lobby. Her back was to him, but he would recognize her backside anywhere.

As if realizing that someone was staring at her, she turned her head. Her face brightened when she saw him. Finishing up her conversation, she rushed over to him and planted an affectionate kiss on his cheek, "Hey, stranger."

"You look good today."

He followed Lexi to her office while she talked along the way, "You aren't going to believe it, but I have a pooch, nothing noticeable, but it is there."

Before he could answer, she had shut her office door and grabbed his hand and placed it on her stomach, "I still can't believe that there is a tiny human being growing right here."

He didn't know what he was supposed to feel, but as he looked into her eyes he found himself at a complete loss for words. His heart swelled with longing, if only he had been the one to marry her years ago. He wished it was his baby she was carrying. He regretted not telling her years ago how he felt. Perhaps if he had things would be different today.

For a fleeting moment, he wanted to lean down and kiss her, but he stopped himself. As she looked up into his eyes, he saw the same longing that he felt. This woman was a temptress; the overwhelming attraction he felt for her was an utter distraction. He told himself that he should not, could not, take her into his arms and kiss her. He had to control this overpowering magnetism that had him gravitating towards her.

In the next moment, he did something he absolutely should not be doing. Something he'd wanted to do for a while now, something that could lead to nothing but trouble -he could no longer hold himself back, he kissed her. Her lips moved into his, tempting the last bit of control he had left.

The moment his lips touched hers, he forgot about why he thought this was such a bad idea. Her lips were warm and inviting as he brushed his lips back and forth over hers, savoring the feeling. There was a moment of hesitancy to the kiss before it turned demanding and passionate. He was surprised by the instant effect her body had on him. Her eyes looked up at him as her lips parted, begging to be kissed once more. He ran his hands through her hair. The silkiness felt like pure heaven against his skin.

He wanted her to forget about Bennett. He only wanted her to know that his heart burned with desire for her.

As his mouth continued to move over hers, his tongue commanded hers. He tasted every sensual spot as she moaned with pleasure. That little sound was all it took for his resolve to break. "You are too tempting of a woman," he whispered huskily in her ear.

- - - - - - - - - ● - - - - - - - - - -

Those words broke any resolve she had left. Her mind may tell her to stop, but her body told her that she could not let this moment pass. Besides, she needed to be wanted, even for a moment. She deserved some pleasure in her life, to feel passion and pure lust. There would be no strings attached, and she knew that Kyle was not looking for a commitment from her. One time would be enough to satisfy her hunger, and to quiet her hormones.

She found her hands moving up his chest and felt his heart pound ferociously in his chest. She wrapped her arms around his neck, pressing her body firmly against his. Her eyes sparkled with passion.

- - - - - - - - - ● - - - - - - - - -

His blood began to boil at the mere thought of Bennett putting his hands on this woman, caressing her enticing curves. Jealousy flowed through him at the thought of how his friend devoured her sweet mouth with his bruising kisses. He wanted to be the only man who had felt those lips, tasted her sweetness.

This was not right; he should stop himself. She was still vulnerable. But there was no imagining Lexi's eager response to him. She was every bit as aroused as he was; she wanted him as much as he wanted her.

The sparks between the two were undeniable. Her body language was inviting, and passion burned in her eyes.

As he kissed her again, he found himself wanting more. She was like an addictive poison. Their kiss deepened as passion ignited deep inside of him. The sexual tension that had been brewing underneath the surface came rushing through. The kiss went from hot to sweltering in a matter of seconds.

His hands slid down her back and pulled her closer to his body. As the realization entered his sex-starved brain about what he was doing, he backed away from her. She surprised him by pulling him closer to her.

He often wondered what it would feel like if she touched him. His dreams were not near as good as the real thing. He looked deeply into her eyes, not caring if the desire he felt for this woman showed on his face.

- - - - - - ● - ● ● - - - - - -

Lexi heard her heart pounding in her ears. She was not sure what came over her.

She felt so desired and wanted. Kyle was reminding her that she was a woman, a very desirable woman. Before her mind could drift back to what her life was like with Bennett, she told herself to stop it; memories of him would get her nowhere.

"Are you sure about this?"

His question penetrated her fogged brain and went straight to her heart. She needed something to ease the pain that Bennett left in her heart. She needed to know she could satisfy a man. Tomorrow, she would deal with the consequences.

She gazed up at him with passion shimmering in her eyes. It was the most passionate yearning he had ever seen in a woman. The heat showing in his eyes ignited her blood. "Is this something you want?"

After kissing him passionately, she told him, "I want to feel alive. I need to know Bennett was wrong, and I am not frigid. That I can please a man."

Those words caused his blood to heat and race through his body. In an instant, his lips devoured hers with a fiery passion that was hotter than any flame.

"Lexi, you take my breath away, I never thought it would be like this."

"Neither did I," she gasped.

"You are so beautiful. So tempting. So desirable." He filled her with all of him, "I can't seem to control myself."

As he brought her to the brink of pleasure, his hands roamed over her body, stroking, and caressing. Sex has never been this good; no one has ever brought her so much pleasure or made her feel this desirable.

He placed a palm against her still flushed cheek, "About what happened just now…"

She placed a finger on his lips, stopping the words before they could ruin the moment, "We both wanted this. We are two grown adults who had a need and fulfilled it. You did something for me that no one else has ever done; you made me feel desirable. I don't want this to ruin our friendship, it means too much to me. Let's just say tonight was a small detour in our lives."

Chapter 11

A new day. A new start. But she was not nervous about this new start. She was actually looking forward to it, ready for, possibly anxious, about the prospect of moving on. It was time. She had a new house and was ready to forget the past.

There was a garden she could lose herself in. Lexi actually found herself interested in something that wasn't work, and now that she was expecting a baby, she could almost imagine her future. Besides, whether she was ready or not, she would soon be a mom.

And this was the day, the day that she would start her new life, and get prepared to welcome her baby. She had made arrangements previously with Bennett for her to move her belongings out of the house they once shared, and into her new house. Thankfully, all that she had remaining in the house was stacked in the spare room, carefully packed in moving boxes.

With the help of Jason and her dad, it hadn't taken them long to load everything in the moving truck she had rented. She did not want any of the furniture her and Bennett had bought as a married couple – in all honesty, she did not want anything her and Bennett had bought together. All she wanted was belongings she had bought, or that had been given to her by friends and family.

As Lexi pulled away from the house, she was leaving the past behind her and driving to her future. A future full of excitement and uncertainty.

Jason and her dad were behind her in the moving van. Once they were at the house, Lexi walked over to the van, "I really do appreciate your help."

Her dad opened the back of the van and told her, "It's no problem. You just tell us where you want the boxes."

"We can stack the boxes in the spare room. I'll go through them little by little."

Several hours later they finally had the moving van unloaded. Her dad had offered to return the rental on the way home, and Lexi had gladly accepted.

As they drove off, her phone rang. She glanced at the screen before deciding to take the call. It was her best friend Christi.

"Hey, woman, what's up?"

"I was just calling to see how you were doing."

"I'm doing all right. Taking it one day at a time."

"You sound tired."

"No, just still angry. But, today was better than yesterday."

"Did y'all get everything moved in okay?"

"Finally. Dad and Jason just left."

"I'm sure you're tired, so I will let you go. I'll call you again tomorrow, okay?"

"You know, you don't have to check up on me every day. I'll be fine."

For a moment there was nothing but silence. "I am worried about you. I care about you and want to make sure that you are okay."

"I appreciate it, but really, I'll be okay."

After the two friends hung up, Lexi let out a long sigh. She appreciated everyone's concern, but she really would get through this.

Chapter 12

It was a beautiful morning, so Lexi decided to take a walk downtown. The fresh air would do her some good. A diverse group of shops, boutiques, and restaurants lined downtown Springport. Several food and drink vendors were set up around downtown selling sausage po-boys, crawfish étouffée, gumbo and snow cones.

As she window-shopped, she noticed people milling around. It seemed as if all around her were couples walking hand in hand, friends arm in arm, and children laughing as they danced around their parents.

Just as she turned around to go home, she saw Kyle walking her way.

"I'm surprised to see you downtown."

"I was in the mood for some beignets and café au lait, so I was headed to the café on First Street. Care to join me?"

"I was on my way home."

"Come on, it is right around the corner. We can walk back to your car, eating and talking on our way."

"Okay, but you are buying."

Laughing, he replied, "Deal."

After they purchased their beignets and coffee, he walked her back to her car. Once there, she said disappointingly, "Well, I guess I better get home. Thanks again for the beignets and coffee."

"No problem. Call me if you need anything."

- - - • • • • • ● • • • • • • - - -

As she drove up to the house, she noticed Bennett's car sitting in the driveway and groaned. "What is he doing here?"

The day had started off perfectly, and she was not in the mood to deal with him. The man infuriated her lately. His latest personality flaw was that he wanted all of life's privileges, but none of the responsibilities. On top of that, her baby bump had become more pronounced, and she still had not told him he would soon be a father.

When Bennett saw her pull into her driveway, he got out of his car. She asked him rather harshly, "What are you doing here?"

"Maybe I just wanted to pay my wife a visit."

"Please, you don't do anything unless there is an ulterior motive."

Placing a hand over his heart, he feigned surprise, "I'm hurt. Maybe I want a reconciliation."

She let out a short laugh, "Please, I know you. Something is up. It has been twelve weeks since you informed me you wanted a divorce, that you found someone who you loved."

"Maybe I realized I made a mistake and that my life is nothing without you."

"Save the crap for someone who believes it. Now, what do you want?"

"Okay, I need to speed the divorce along. April is pregnant, and she wants to get married before she shows."

Lexi felt the ground opening up underneath her. His words were a kick in the gut, a knife straight to her heart. "You can't be serious?"

"You must have realized things were over between the two of us." Giving her a pitiful look he said, "You have to accept that I am with another woman. I love April and we want to get married. I never even considered having kids, and now, I have a pregnant girlfriend."

She gritted her teeth at his conceit. The thought of April fooling around on him became almost too much for her to hold in, and she had to bite back a laugh. Instead, she found some inner courage. *Well, here goes nothing*, "Well, guess what buddy, you not only have a pregnant mistress, but also a pregnant wife."

"What are you talking about?"

"I'm four months pregnant."

Bennett looked at her with murderous rage in his eyes. "You conniving little bitch. What did you do? Did you stop taking the pill so that you could trap me in this marriage?" Grabbing her arm, he gave her a good shake, "I don't care how you do it, but I want this pregnancy terminated! Do you hear me?"

Startled by his reaction, she replied, "Wait a second. It's not like I was exactly expecting this news either, especially since my husband had just left me for another woman. As far as this baby goes, I don't need anything from you. I have a stable career and am perfectly capable of raising this child on my own. I can provide everything he or she needs." The last thing this child needed was a reluctant father; besides, it was Bennett's loss. She refused to terminate this pregnancy.

Pointing her finger and jabbing his chest with it, "And if you think that I am getting an abortion, you have another thing coming, buddy. I will NOT end the life of a child growing inside of me."

Bennett surmised, "You and I both know that we married way too fast. Neither of us knew what the other person was like. Having a child together is the last thing we need. I'm telling you right now that I want this pregnancy terminated. One pregnant woman is enough, and I don't need it to be you. I plan on having a happy marriage with April, and I don't need your ass messing it up."

"I agree that we married too fast; we were both caught up in the magic of the moment." She left out that while the sex was great; a marriage could not survive off of just good sex.

She no longer even recognized this man she had married. He was an entirely different individual. When they married she was an idealist, she actually believed in the institution of marriage, but twelve weeks ago she became a realist. There was no way for their marriage to survive, and she knew it. He was in love with another woman, a much younger woman, who was also pregnant. Instead of feeling sad, she felt liberated. It felt as if a great burden had been lifted off of her shoulders. She did not regret her pregnancy either. She could handle this pregnancy and she would be an excellent mother. This might be her only chance to have a child, even if Bennett was the father. She vehemently replied, "You better listen up, Benny boy! If you think that you can strong arm me into terminating this pregnancy, you have another thing coming. A living human being is growing inside of me, one that I plan to love with all my heart. I could care less if you are part of this child's life or not, but I will keep this baby."

Waving his hands in surrender, he asked, "If an abortion is out of the question, how about adoption?"

Lexi was furious with Bennett. He did not want any acknowledgment of this child. "No! I will do no such thing." Lexi looked him directly in the eyes, "I already love this baby. I am keeping it, with or without your help."

He glared at her, "Lots of women give up their babies for adoption. It would be the best thing for all of us. No one would think less of you."

"I have no problems with other women putting their babies up for adoption, but I am not other women. I can afford to take care of this child without you. I will provide for this child no matter how tough it gets."

Knowing that he would not change her mind, he stormed off. After Bennett had left, she called her lawyer to see if there was any way they could hurry this divorce along. She explained to the attorney that the fate of her marriage had remained unchanged. However, her husband's mistress was pregnant, and they wanted to get married as soon as possible. "I believe this may give us the leverage we need to have him sign the proposed changes in the divorce settlement."

The attorney agreed, "You could be right. I will call his lawyer today and try to push this through. I don't see a problem if the divorce is uncontested, there are no children and very few assets to divide."

Lexi did not even correct him about any children being involved. She did not want this child being the reason the divorce did not go through. "Great, let me know. I'm ready to wash my hands of this whole matter."

Chapter 13

As she stood in front of her bathroom mirror, she surveyed her reflection. Turning to her side, she looked at her stomach and saw a slight bulge to it. She ran her hands over her growing stomach and smiled. Seeing the bulge made this whole thing seem very real.

She had read that the baby was now the size of an apple. As she looked at her reflection, she had to admit it did look as if she indeed swallowed a whole apple. She would soon have to buy new clothes since a number of hers were becoming too tight around the waist.

As she finished getting dressed, she could barely contain her excitement.   She would see her baby today.

- - - - - - - - ● - - - - - - - - - -

Once at the doctor's office, it was as if time was moving in slow motion as she waited for the nurse to call her back. As Lexi sat and watched the couples sitting together, a feeling of intense loneliness overcame her. She wistfully wished someone was here with her. That there was someone to share the wonder of the experience with, and rejoice with her when she heard the heartbeat. The birth of the baby deserved fanfare and celebration. Parents that loved it and could not wait for the birth.

Once in the exam room, she lifted her shirt and unbuttoned her pants. Her breath caught as Dr. Allen squirted the warm, goopy liquid on her stomach. Before starting, he asked the nurse to dim the lights, "Okay, before we start, do you want to know the sex?"

Shaking her head, she said, "No, I want to be surprised."

Laughing, he told her, "That is a first for me. Not too many women want to be surprised anymore."

As a computer monitor in front of her came to life, the tiny exam room was filled with a sound similar to a heartbeat emitting from the monitor. Dr. Allen looked over at her, "That is your baby's heartbeat you are hearing." With a wave of his hand, "And here is your baby."

Her eyes were fixed on the monitor as he passed the ultrasound probe across her lower abdomen. The baby was so tiny, but she could make out its little fingers and toes. She really did have this little person growing inside of her.

As she stared at the screen, the doctor took measurements and talked about several different things, but all she could focus on was the baby.

After the doctor had finished studying the image, he picked up a towel and wiped the ultrasound jelly off of her tummy. "The baby is very healthy. It looks as if you are five months pregnant."

She was sitting up on the exam table now. "Everything looks okay with the baby?"

"Perfect. I know you said the baby's daddy is not in the picture, but you may want to ask a close family member or friend to be your coach. You don't want to go through this alone unless you have no other choice. Also, I need you to stop by the nurse's desk so that she can direct you to where you go for your blood work. Once that is done, we will make your next appointment."

As she was leaving, the nurse gave her a picture of her baby. She was just so excited. She scheduled her next appointment in four weeks. She hoped everyone was correct, and time would fly by.

Once in her car, she took out the ultrasound picture and beamed. It was actual proof that a life was growing inside of her. She ran her hands along the image. Tiny feet, tiny hands. She held back tears threatening to spill. If only she had someone with her to share this joyous moment with.

She could have asked Kyle, he would have gladly come. But she already took up too much of his time; it would not be fair to him.

Feeling lonely, she picked up the phone and called Kyle. With the divorce almost finalized, she found herself fantasizing about him more often. Besides the baby, he seemed to be the only other person she thought about lately. In the past, she'd had romantic feelings for him, but he never seemed to be interested in her. Now with her failed marriage behind her, she began to wonder if maybe he shared those same feelings. However, their friendship was too precious to chance it. She did not know what she would do if she lost Kyle as a friend.

She hastily told him when he answered, "I saw the baby for the first time."

"By the sound of your voice, you are very excited."

She replied, "I am, and I was wondering if you wanted to meet me for lunch at Clementine's. There is something I need to talk to you about."

"I can do that."

- - - - - - - - - ● - - - - - - - - - -

Kyle wondered what she wanted to talk about. When he arrived at the restaurant, he saw her waiting at their favorite table. Waving at him, she said, "I went ahead and ordered us the shrimp and crab fondue."

"Sounds good. You look like you are feeling a lot better."

"I am. The morning sickness is pretty much gone."

"You have more color to your cheeks."

"I even have a little more of a pooch. I have to go shopping and buy some clothes that fit. Most of my pants and skirts won't even close, and I am wearing dresses that are being tested to their maximum stretching limits."

Laughing at her, he joked, "And I am sure that you dread shopping."

Shaking her head, she jokingly said, "I despise shopping. And I am not looking forward to this particular shopping trip. No woman wants to purchase bigger clothes."

"Would you like company?"

Before she could answer, she stood up and placed his hand on her stomach, "The baby has started to move. I'm not sure if you can feel it, but it feels like there are tiny butterflies in my stomach."

He could tell that there was a bump starting to show on her stomach, but he wasn't sure what he was supposed to feel. As she sat back down, he found himself at a complete loss for words. When he looked into her eyes, his heart swelled with longing. If only he had been the one to marry her years ago. He wished it was his baby she was carrying. He should have told her years ago how he felt, then maybe things would be different today.

When the waitress stopped by to take Kyle's drink order and see if they were ready to order lunch, she stopped his mind from wandering where it should not. They both ordered the special; margarita chicken with roasted potatoes and snap beans.

"So, what's going on with you right now? Other than the pregnancy, of course."

"We have a lot to catch up on. Bennett stopped by the house the other day to let me know that April is also expecting a baby."

"You are kidding."

"Nope. Not only that, but he wants to know if we can speed the divorce along faster."

"So, what did you tell him?"

"Well, after I let him know that I was also pregnant, I told him I had no problem with a speedy divorce."

As he watched her facial expressions, his heart warmed a little more for this woman. He asked, "And how did he take the news about your pregnancy?"

"To say that he was shocked would be putting it mildly."

"How do you feel about this whole situation?"

She rubbed her face with both hands, and then let out her breath on an exhausted sigh. She replied, "It is sinking in that I am pregnant. I came to grips weeks ago that Bennett and I are done. I won't stay with a man who cheats on me, or that wants me to terminate my baby."

"Good for you. So, all that remains is the pregnancy details."

"Yes, and that is why I wanted to talk to you."

"Oh yeah. I'm not an expert on pregnancy."

She laughed. "You are so silly at times. No, I wanted to ask you how you would feel about being my coach during this pregnancy. I could ask my mom, possibly even my sister-in-law or brother, but I think we would butt heads more than anything. Mom is constantly telling me that I should forgive Bennett and get back together for the baby. That won't happen, even if his soon to be wife wasn't pregnant."

"Stick to your guns on that. I would be honored to be your coach, whatever that means."

"Well, you may want to think about it. You have to be there for the birth."

"Even if I wasn't your coach, I would be there for you. I refuse to let you go through this alone."

She reached across the table and squeezed his hand. "Thank you so much. You have always been there for me."

Chapter 14

Two weeks after signing the lease on her new home, Lexi stood in the middle of the living room and surveyed the stack of boxes, all neatly taped shut and labeled with their contents. As Lexi tried to decide what she wanted to tackle first, she rubbed her belly and told the baby, "Don't worry, you're going to love this new home. There is a yard for you to play in when you get bigger, and I'm certain there are children in the neighborhood to play with."

Lexi did not miss the house she and Bennett had shared. There were too many negative emotions attached to it. She dropped her head in dismay. *Stop it, Bennett was your life, but not your whole life.* It was hard to accept that their marriage had been a lie. Her whole marriage. She was uncertain how to deal with the anger, the betrayal, and the humiliation she felt. Was there something wrong with her or did she simply have awful taste when it came to picking a man?

Enough of this she told herself. She could not spend her days brooding and bitter.

This house represented a fresh start, a new chapter in her life.

Even better, this new chapter included a baby that she had dreamed about for so long. It did not matter that Bennett did not want anything to do with the child's life. She was fully prepared to raise a child on her own.

Lexi was so deep in thought that the knocking at her front door startled her. Looking out the window, she recognized the car in her driveway.

Lexi opened the door and hugged Janie, Madison, and Grant. "This is a pleasant surprise."

"We thought you could use a little help. Besides, your mom had mentioned that she was going to come over today and I thought you could use the extra company."

"You are the best." Blowing Janie a kiss, "Thank you. Jason and dad moved the heavy items, but I would appreciate any help I can get unpacking all the boxes."

As Lexi showed her sister-in-law the new house, Janie said excitedly, "I love this house." She turned to her children, "Now why don't you two go outside and play while we unpack."

Rushing to the back door, they replied in unison, "Yes ma'am.

As they unpacked boxes, Janie confided, "I am so proud of the courage you had to dump that two-timing husband of yours." Looking around, "And this house is just so perfect for you. It suits your personality."

Lexi agreed, "I know right. It is perfect."

She looked out the window and watched the children play in the backyard, "I love hearing them laugh and watching them play outside."

"They are great kids, and play so well together. Jason and I constantly fought."

Janie sighed, "Yes, Jason has mentioned on several occasions how y'all didn't get along. Sometimes, I think it bothers him that he tormented you the way he did."

Lexi put her hands on her hips, and said in mock sarcasm, "Well, you wouldn't know it by the way he treats me now."

Smirking, "Well, part of him has never forgiven you for the chocolate prank."

Lexi burst into laughter. She had completely forgotten about giving him a chocolate laxative. When Lexi was fifteen, Jason decided to fill her dresser drawers full of frogs. Lexi decided to get even. Her brother loved chocolate, and if he saw it lying around the house – he claimed it as his. So Lexi, in all of her infinite wisdom, placed some chocolate laced with a laxative in a bowl on her nightstand with a note, "Hands off Jason!" The temptation had been too great and Jason took the chocolate. Only Jason did not eat the chocolate right away, as Lexi had planned. Instead, Jason waited until the next morning to eat the chocolate and it was while at the bus stop. While eating the chocolate, he relentlessly teased Lexi. "Mm, sis, this has to be the best chocolate." He stuck his chocolate coated tongue out at her, "Too bad there isn't enough for you to have any."

"You are a brat, Jason!"

This time the joke was on her brother - who despised using the restrooms at school and would rush home afterward to relieve himself. Unfortunately, the laxative started working faster than she had anticipated. Jason's stomach began gurgling on the bus ride to school. When they arrived at school, Jason knew he could not call home and say he was sick. That was forbidden - their dad had one hard fast rule – they had better be bleeding and dying before they called him to come home sick. An upset stomach did not qualify by any means.

"Lexi, I don't feel good. I think that chocolate was bad."

"That is what you get for eating something that did not belong to you, piggy."

With sweat beading on his forehead, "Sis, I don't think I'm going to make it to school much less to the end of the day."

His stomach let out a loud gurgle, "Ugh, I think I'm going to crap all over myself." Holding his stomach, "I can feel it peak-a-booing." Giving his sister an evil glare, "I'm serious.   I may not make it to the bathroom."

Lexi's punishment had been so severe that she decided no practical joke was worth it, no matter how warranted she felt it was.

"I was getting even with him for putting frogs in my underwear drawer."

"I'm just glad my two aren't like y'all were."

Slightly irritated, Lexi responded, "Shoo, Jason could actually use some grief in his life."

She shrugged, "Girl, my husband is a hopeless case."

"I wish he would understand why I am divorcing Bennett."

"He is a man, but he does have a good heart. However, he has a hard time showing his emotions. He also doesn't like to admit when he is wrong, and if he acknowledges your divorce, he has to admit he was wrong about Bennett."

"I think we both have problems admitting when we have made a mistake," Lexi confessed.

Her sister-in-law swiped her hands together, "Enough of this soul-searching talk. What else do we need to do here?" She walked around the house and commented, "The kitchen, dining room and bedrooms are done."

Lexi nodded her head, "Yeah, I think all that is left is to figure out where to put the knickknacks and hang the pictures."

Janie picked up her water bottle and took a sip, "All right, let's get this finished, and then we will order a pizza."

"Sounds like a plan."

When the knock sounded at the door, Janie and Lexi looked at each other and said in unison, "She's here."

Lexi went to greet her guest and opened the front door, "Hey, Mom."

Lexi's mom held her hands to the side, with her palms up, and asked, "Why in the heck did you move to this house?"

Lexi tried to hide her disappointment, "Mom, the house is not that bad. I find it charming."

Her mom shook her head as she stepped inside. "Well, I hope your rent isn't that much. This house needs a lot of work." As her mom surveyed the house, Lexi rubbed her forehead. Not only was her mom already complaining about the house, but she came dressed in long pants, a silk blouse, and black high heels. There was no way that her mom planned to help unpack boxes today. The only reason she came was to check out Lexi's new house.

Clicking her tongue, "The house you had with Bennett was so much nicer."

Janie came to her defense, "Oh, no, this house is much cozier. It suits Lexi perfectly."

Before anyone could say anything else, Grant and Madison came rushing in. Both children gave their grandma hugs. Madison tugged on her grandmother's shirt, "MiMi, MiMi." The young girl demanded, "Look what I can do." Madison opened her mouth, stuck out her tongue, and wiggled her front tooth. "Mom says the tooth fairy will be coming to see me soon. I can't wait."

Lexi could see her mom shudder. She had to hold back a laugh. Growing up, her mom did not like when any of her children had a loose tooth. If they could not pull it out themselves, then it was her dad's responsibility.

Lexi's mother tousled Madison's hair, "That's so exciting, sweetheart." She looked at both of her grandchildren and smiled, "Now, what have you two been up to today? From the looks of you, I'd say a lot of fun playing outside."

Grant eagerly nodded his head up and down, "MiMi, we found all kinds of rocks in the garden."

"Oh really, why don't you show them to me?"

Lexi let out a sigh of relief. Perhaps the children would keep her mother entertained where she would not constantly nag Lexi on the house.

After the children had shown their grandmother the rocks they had collected, Grant shoved them back into his jean pocket and told her, "MiMi, we're gonna go outside and play some more." As they rushed out the back door, they waved goodbye.

Her mom stood up, walked over to the kitchen cabinet, and glided a finger along it.

As Lexi's mom inspected the kitchen, Janie announced, "I think I will put on a pot of coffee."

Lexi's mom nodded her head, "That sounds wonderful, my dear."

Lexi helped Janie brew a pot of coffee. While they prepared the coffee, Lexi's mom stated, "I think I will start cleaning up in here, after we have had our coffee. I can at least sweep the floors and wash the cabinets down." She motioned with a wide wave of her hand.

Lexi's eyebrows rose in surprise, "You will?"

Lexi took in her mom's freshly lacquered nails, clothes, and high heels. *This should be interesting.* She thought to herself

"I told you I would come help. I'm here, aren't I?"

Lexi walked over and gave her mom a hug, "Thank you. I really do appreciate your help." And Lexi really did mean it.

"Think nothing of it, sweetie." She placed a finger under Lexi's chin and scrutinized her face, "By the way, you really do need to do something about the bags under your eyes." Her brow puckered. "You are not getting enough sleep."

Lexi did not bother to comment. Janie handed each woman a cup of coffee, "Here you go. Drink up before it gets cold."

Chapter 15

Lexi picked at the lettuce on her plate and grimaced. Two hours ago, it would not have been considered appetizing, but now it was plain repulsive. She was trying to eat healthier, but this was not what she craved. Picking up her plate, she dumped the salad into the trash before putting the plate into the dishwasher.

Sitting back at the kitchen bar, she opened her laptop and pulled up her calendar. It was a busy month at the hotel; she had two weddings, a retirement party, an anniversary, and a real estate convention just this week alone.

Unable to concentrate on work, she walked over to the refrigerator for a snack. Scowling at the state of her refrigerator and pantry, she reminded herself that she had to go shopping. There was a box of cereal, but no milk. She did not even have peanut butter in her house. Some parent she was turning out to be. She needed to do a better job of keeping the house stocked with food.

As she took out a yogurt, her phone rang. She groaned when she saw that the incoming call was from the last person she wanted to talk to, Bennett. Most of the time he called to remind her of which bills she needed to pay. Regardless of what he needed, he made sure to mention what he considered to be her failures as a wife. She was tempted to let the call go straight to voicemail, but he would continue calling until she answered the phone.

She impatiently asked, "What Bennett?"

"My divorce attorney drew up the revisions to the divorce papers and will send them to your attorney."

She planned on making the cheapskate pay as much in legal fees as she could. She had no intention of making this easy for him. She wanted to make the final decision on the terms of the divorce.

"I have a busy week at the hotel, but I will get with my attorney and see what he thinks."

"You don't need to waste time reviewing the documents; I did as you suggested. The house is going in my name, and I will pay you for your half. As far as the bills, we will split everything down the middle."

If he thought she would split any bills he obtained while screwing his girlfriend, he was sadly mistaken. She had no intentions of paying anything on the credit card that he charged with regards to HER. He could go straight to hell before she paid one red cent for his cheating bills.

But, of course with Bennett, it was about the money. With him, everything was always about money.

By the time they hung up, her hands were shaking. Just as she was getting ready to run to the store and buy out their chocolate, there was a knock at her door. Fearing it was Bennett, she peeked out the peephole, and her heart skipped a beat. She opened the door with a big smile, "You always know when I need cheering up."

Kyle gave her a kiss, "Uh oh. That doesn't sound good."

Exasperated, she told him. "I just had a run-in with Bennett."

"So that was why your calls went straight to voicemail. I came by to see if you wanted to grab a bite to eat?"

She moaned in delight, "A good burger and a chocolate shake sounds divine right now. Let me go freshen up before we leave."

In the bathroom, Lexi splashed water on her face. She placed a hand on her stomach and surveyed her image. She let out a sigh of relief. Although she felt nauseous, she looked presentable. No one would be able to tell the inner turmoil she was dealing with.

As Kyle helped her into his car, he stated, "I know just where to take you. The Roadrunner has the best burgers."

When they entered the small hamburger joint, she noticed that it was packed with teenagers. Kyle spotted a vacant table near the back and led her over to it before someone else could snatch it up.

As they made themselves comfortable at the table, the waitress came over to hand them menus, "Do you know what you want to drink?"

He smiled up at the waitress, "Can we please have two chocolate shakes?"

"Coming right up."

While the waitress went to fill their drink order, Lexi continued to look over the menu. A few minutes later the waitress set down their chocolate shakes, she asked, "Have you decided on what you would like to order?"

Lexi looked over the menu before deciding, "I want the bacon cheddar burger with fries, please."

As the waitress jotted down her order, Kyle replied, "I would like the Buffalo Burger and a large order of onion rings."

Lexi looked over at Kyle, "I didn't see that burger."

"It is over on the chicken side. It is delicious. They take a jalapeño chicken patty, cook it and then coat it in hot sauce. They top it with blue cheese and shavings of celery."

Her mouth watered just from the description. "Now you have me wanting that instead."

His eyes twinkled with mischief, "I can be persuaded to share my burger with you but hands off my onion rings. You are the one who ordered plain old fries."

She laughed at his antics. "Well, that's okay; I wasn't planning on sharing my fries with you."

The waitress quickly appeared with their order. As she set the food down, Lexi's eyes widened, "This is a lot of food."

Without responding to Lexi's comment, the waitress asked, "Can I get y'all anything else?"

They both shook their heads, so the waitress moved onto the next table. As Lexi bit into her burger, Kyle squirted ketchup onto his plate. He hovered the bottle over her plate and waited for a response. With a mouth full of the best burger she had ever had, she nodded.

Picking up a french fry, she dragged it through the ketchup and moaned in appreciation, "This is pure heaven. You know where to go for the best food."

Laughing as he replied, "One day I saw teenagers flocking to this place. I figured if that many kids congregated here, the food was either really good or extremely cheap. I decided to take a chance."

Waving a french fry in the air, she said, "Well, what a great friend you turned out to be. How can you keep a place like this hidden from me? You know how much I enjoy food!"

Shrugging his shoulders, he said, "Something tells me that Bennett wouldn't come here anyway."

"No, you are right. He is more of a fancy linens, glasses on the table, and dim lighting kind of guy." Savoring another bite of her burger she continued, "But he doesn't know what he is missing."

As she took another bite, she thought about how a crisp, salty french fry and the tangy, sweet ketchup were the perfect marriage of food. She had always had a deep, abiding love for food. The crispier, sweeter and greasier the better in her opinion, and if she went by her cravings, her child would have the same love for food.

Knowing Lexi as well as he did, Kyle knew something had upset her earlier, "So what had your panties in a bunch today?"

Rolling her eyes, she replied, "You even have to ask that. I hate talking about Bennett in front of you, but I swear that man is out to drive me insane."

Kyle reached across the table and squeezed her hand, "I may be friends with Bennett, but you have always been there for me, and I will be here for you. Besides,

Bennett and I haven't talked much lately. I think he believes he is too good for me."

"Yeah, he doesn't understand why after selling your company you would want to do something like fishing charters. It irks him that you are more successful in your career than him. You both went to school for the same thing, but he is still working for a computer programming company, and you have already bought and sold a company. He is hoping you fail at your next business."

Shrugging his shoulders nonchalantly he said, "It's not my fault that the man doesn't have any drive or ambition.   Bennett is good at riding someone's shirttails and then stealing that person's thunder. He always wanted praise and recognition rather than taking the bull by the horns and doing a good job."

"Yeah, you are right. I hope April is ready to work her derriere off. The way Bennett likes to spend money, she will soon find out that I was the money train. One of the reasons he wants the divorce finalized is because I opened my own account at a different bank. He honestly thought I would agree to split the bills in half plus pay him alimony. My attorney has everything showing two of the credit cards were in his name only. And the credit card we had in both of our names he used for hotels and meals to wine and dine his mistress."

"Oh baby, I like when you get all feisty."

"I have decided not to let Bennett roll all over me. If he thinks he will get a simple divorce and have me continue to pay his way, he has another thing coming. While married, I may have been blinded by my love for him and had no problem letting him go through money like it was water, but those days are long gone. If he wants to keep living large, he needs to pay his own way."

"You are wise letting your attorney go over everything with a fine-tooth comb. I wouldn't just agree to whatever he has in the papers either."

"No, I won't let him bully me into anything. I thought when we said 'I do' it would be forever, but if he thinks I will let him and April have that life without a little misery, he has another thing coming to him. I refuse to finance his new life with her."

"I am proud of you for standing your ground."

"I worry this is all portraying me to be a bitter ex-wife. I thought I would have a long and happy marriage. When I said my wedding vows, I thought it was forever, and now, I am walking into the unknown alone."

"At least you found out now instead of later. Can you imagine living your life only to find out forty years from now that he never loved you?"

Shaking her head, she said sadly, "No, I couldn't. I just wish I had known he was playing the field. I had the doctor run all kinds of blood work since the idiot more than likely never wore protection. I sometimes wonder if there is such a thing as happily ever after. My parents are still together, but Mom tends to make Dad's life a living hell. I don't understand how he can grin and bear her constant put-downs. He just puts up with her crap."

"Maybe he sees her as she was. Something tells me that she wasn't always that way."

"She has been that way for as long as I can remember. They say love is blind, and perhaps, in his eyes, it is."

Kyle thought back on his childhood, "My parents have always been happy. Even after all this time, they are crazy in love; yet, they can't understand why I haven't settled down. Mom constantly reminds me that she would like to be a grandmother while she can still enjoy it."

Kyle lived in the moment and always would. She, on the other hand, wanted to know what her future entailed.

- - - - - - - - ● - - - - - - - -

On the drive back to her house, she thought about her life. Perhaps it was time for her to change her own outlook.

As he walked her to her front door, she asked, "Would you like to come in for a cup of coffee?"

Not wanting the night to end, he said, "A cup of coffee sounds perfect."

In the kitchen, she asked, "Did you want a latte or just a cup of coffee?"

"Coffee is fine."

As she waited for the coffee to finish, she gathered the mugs, cream, and sugar. Calling out towards the living room, she said, "Did you want flavored creamer?"

From the kitchen door, he asked, "What flavors do you have?"

"I have caramel, amaretto, and crème brûlée."

"Surprise me."

She poured them each a cup of coffee with the crème brûlée creamer. Handing him his cup of coffee, they walked into the living room to make themselves comfortable.

Over coffee, they talked about how their day went.

- - - - - - ●● ● ●● - ● - ● - - - -

As Kyle was leaving Lexi gave him a hug goodnight. He slowly placed his hands gently on her back and turned his face away from her hair, not wanting to inhale its tantalizing smell. He consciously did not lean into her embrace and kept his body away from her curves.

She was everything he wanted, but she was not his to have.

Moving his hands to her shoulders, he stepped back and put distance between them. With a heavy heart, he forced a smile at her. "Goodnight, Lexi. Sweet dreams."

Kissing his cheek, "Goodnight Kyle. Drive safe."

As he drove home, he considered how brave Lexi was. She was determined to raise this baby even though Bennett was being an imbecile. How could a father refuse to acknowledge a child he helped conceive?

No, he was wrong. Lexi would not be doing this alone. He had known her family for longer than he could remember. While not a close-knit family at times, they were there for each other. She would be able to lean on them when times got tough.

Chapter 16

Lexi was walking to her office when she saw her mother-in-law, Marlene Daigle, walk through the doors. She inwardly scowled. Thankfully, she had time to school her face into a pleasant mask before talking to her mother-in-law. Although short, she was still an imposing woman with piercing eyes and jet black hair that came from a bottle. It sat ratted to its fullest and piled in a neatly coiffed bun on top of her head. Her face was caked with makeup and as usual, the blue eyeshadow highlighted the clown-like style.

"Good evening," Lexi said cheerfully. "Was there something I can help you with today?"

Marlene gave her a withering look and stated, "You have something I need."

Lexi looked at her in disbelief, "What in the world could I possibly have that you need?"

Lexi stared at her in dismay as disgust filled the woman's eyes. "I came to get back the jewelry Bennett had given you while he was married to you."

Lexi's jaw hardened, "I gave Bennett back everything, including the wedding ring."

"No, my son informed me that you still had everything. I want it back!"

Lexi tried to control her temper. "Then your son is lying to you. I even had him sign an affidavit listing everything that was returned to him. Afterwards, my divorce attorney had it notarized."

Flustered, she let out a huff, "I never knew what my son saw in you. I'm so glad he is done with the likes of you."

Lexi shrugged her shoulders, "I can say the same thing. I'm glad to have that man gone from my life." Unable to resist, Lexi informed her, "Oh, by the way, I hear congratulations are in order. You're going to be a grandmother twice over. Have you met your new future daughter-in-law?"

From the woman's expression, Lexi could tell she had taken her by surprise. "I didn't come here to discuss Bennett. I came here to tell you I want my jewelry back."

"And, like I said, Bennett has everything."

As she stormed away, Lexi sweetly called out to her, "Congratulations again. Maybe April will give Bennett plenty of children for you to adore – and babysit."

A look of horrified indignation passed across the woman's face. As she left the hotel, Lexi hoped that her soon-to-be ex-mother-in-law gave Bennett a tongue lashing.

As Marlene stormed off, Lexi was so glad to have that miserable witch out of her life along with that useless man she had brought into existence.

Chapter 17

Later on in the week, Kyle received a call from Lexi, "Hey, you! Would you like to go out for supper? I need to take my mind off of my problems for one night and I'm thinking some good Italian food should do the trick." So much for working up the nerve to ask her out, Kyle thought to himself. She had beaten him to the punch.

Kyle had racked his brain most of the afternoon, trying to decide where to take her for dinner. There were several good Italian restaurants in the city, however, he decided on Angelo's. It had the ambiance that he wanted. It was not too romantic, but it would give them privacy.

When he picked her up at the hotel after work, he noticed how tired she looked. He worried that she was pushing herself too hard.

As they arrived at the restaurant, a long line wrapped around the corner of the building. She looked over at him in amazement, "Wow, this place is popular tonight."

Nodding his head, he explained, "They are always busy." Taking her elbow, he escorted her into the restaurant.

The maître d greeted them at the hostess desk, "Good evening, Mr. DuPont, it's good to see you again."

"Good evening, James. I hope your family is doing well."

"Oh, yes sir." Waving his hands, he said, "If you will follow me, your table is ready."

As they walked through the busy restaurant, Kyle noticed how the men turned to stare at Lexi. Without being aware of her actions, she moved her body in a way that begged a guy to come play with it. When she looked at you, the glint in her eyes dared a man to try it. If he could build up the nerve, he would tell her just how he felt about her.

As they were being seated, she teasingly asked, "Do you come here often?"

After the waitress had come by to take their drink orders, he informed her, "I may have been here a few times."

Laughing, she replied, "I kind of figured that since they knew you by sight."

"What can I say, the food is fantastic."

"Well, that's good, because I am famished. Since we were having Italian for supper, I didn't snack a lot this afternoon." She perused the menu with genuine interest. "Everything looks so good."

"I haven't eaten anything here that wasn't good."

"Hmm, are you in the mood for an appetizer? I wonder if their calamari is any good."

"It is. The garlic aioli dipping sauce is out of this world."

"I could go for that. The chicken and shrimp carbonara with pancetta and red peppers sounds divine."

"That sounds good, but I can't pass up the mussels in white wine sauce. It is my favorite dish here."

As they were talking, the waitress came back with their drinks and took their orders.

An uncomfortable silence settled between them. He tried to think of something more to say, but small talk was not his forte. Unlike him, Lexi could carry on simple conversations without difficulty. But he enjoyed listening as she chattered away, and merely responded when prompted.

Unlike most of the women he had dated in the last year or so, Lexi never bored him. While most of the women kept their conversations centered around them, he still found himself disinterested. He at least had the courtesy not to be obvious about it.

For the next two hours, they talked as they ate-she babbled away about random topics, and they laughed.

They even ordered cappuccinos and shared a tiramisu for dessert. Neither could eat a whole dessert, but they were not ready for the night to end.

"Thank you for the wonderful meal and titillating conversation. I needed it."

He gave her a slight smile on his firm lips, "I didn't say much."

She reached up and patted his cheek, "Are you saying that I am a chatterbox?"

"Absolutely not. I am just not much of a talker lately."

On the drive home, they continued to keep the conversation light. He led her to her door to make sure that she made it safely inside, "I really did enjoy dinner. I promise not to talk your ear off next time."

"I'm glad you enjoyed it, and I enjoy listening to what you have to say. We may have to add dinner to our usual dates."

"I would like that, but I don't want to give up our weekly coffees." Standing on her tip toes, she gave him a kiss on the cheek goodnight. He reached for her hands and gave them a quick squeeze before leaving. "I'll give you a call tomorrow and see how you are."

Chapter 18

Lexi looked at her image in the mirror and reinforced, "It will be okay."

She had decided today would be the perfect day to let her family know she was pregnant. The first Sunday of every month it was a tradition to meet at her parents' house for lunch. Her brother Jason would be there, along with his wife, and children. It would be like ripping a Band-Aid off, painful, but over with one swipe.

As Lexi drove to her parents' house, the butterflies in her stomach would not settle down. There was only one way this would end - badly. Knowing her mother, she would reinforce that Lexi to get back together with Bennett. There's no way that would happen, though.

Lexi pulled into her parents' drive, parked her car, and slowly got out. She took slow, deliberate steps to the front door. She wanted to take as long as she could to get there.

With each step Lexi took, she could feel nausea bubbling up inside of her and it was not from the pregnancy. *You can do this. Once this is done, it is done.*

Before Lexi could knock on the door, her mom opened the door and shouted excitedly, "I'm so glad you came. I was worried you wouldn't show."

Lexi groaned, "You know I wouldn't miss lunch with the family."

"I wasn't sure, ever since you decided that divorcing Bennett was the best thing to do, I never know what to expect from you."

"I'm the same Lexi, Mom, I wouldn't miss this tradition for anything."

"Well, honey, come on, let's go inside and get the dinner table ready. Jason should be here soon."

Between the two children, Lexi was positive that Jason was her mom's favorite. They had matching personalities.

She would be considered a true daddy's girl. He seemed to understand her better than anyone else in the family.

As Lexi and her mom were setting the dishes on the table, there was a loud ruckus at the front door. "Hello? Hello, we're here."

Lexi's mom rushed to greet Jason and his family. Family members began hugging each other, and saying, "Hi. How are you?" There was a lot of hugging and kissing as each family member greeted each other.

Jason looked at Lexi, "Looks like you are putting on some weight, Sis. Trying to eat your troubles away?"

Lexi gave her brother an evil eye, "Well, at least I can lose weight, but you will never FIX ugly."

With a shocked expression, Lexi's mother scolded her, "Lexi, that is an awful thing to say. You should be ashamed of yourself."

Jason's wife, Janie, pushed him out of the way and gave Lexi a hug, "Don't pay any attention to that man. He's just being a jerk. I think you look great."

Lexi's mom looked at Jason and said, "I'm so glad you made it. We have the whole family together today. Well, except for Bennett that is."

Lexi had to bite her tongue. It was going to be a challenging day. Lexi's dad walked down the stairs, and said, "I thought I heard someone talking down here." He walked over to Lexi and gave her a big hug, "Are you feeling okay? You look a little down."

Jason scoffed. "Of course she looks down. She doesn't have her husband here. What I think she needs is a reality check."

Jason's wife swatted him, "Now don't you start. This is none of our business, and we are not going to bother Lexi. This is personal, between her and Bennett, and they are the ones who need to work it out."

Jason raised his arms in surrender, "Okay, okay. I'm just saying that things were going along fine until someone decided to get divorced."

Lexi rolled her eyes. Before she could make a comment, her dad broke in, "No ganging up on Lexi. We are supposed to be here today to eat, and be merry, and be grateful that we are alive. Now, I know your mom has cooked something delicious for lunch, and I for one, am starving."

Jason's son, Grant, said, "Papa, I bet I can eat more than you. Mom says I have a hollow leg that never seems to be full."

Laughing, he picked up his grandson and shook his legs. "Yep," holding up the child's left leg, "this leg right here feels as if it needs some food." Looking to his wife, "What do you say we get this boy some food, and try to fill this hollow leg up?"

Laughing, "You are too much. Go sit in the dining room, and the women will bring the food out to you men."

The three women went into the kitchen and started bringing the platters of food to the dining room. Lexi's mom had cooked some of her dad's favorites today. There was chicken stew, rice and gravy, lima beans, honey glazed carrots, hot rolls, and of course, apple dumplings for dessert.

After the platters were set on the table, everyone began fixing their plate. Grace was said, and everyone began eating.

Lexi's dad asked her, "How has work been?"

"Great. Good, but busy."

After everyone had eaten their lunch, and was enjoying their dessert, Lexi said, "Well, I have some news that I wanted to share with you."

Lexi's dad interrupted, "If you are telling us that you're moving to North Carolina permanently, let me enjoy my dessert first."

Jason commented, "Now Dad, why would you automatically assume that Lexi is moving away?"

Lexi's mom chimed in, "We all know that you don't want Lexi to move away, but why don't you wait for Lexi to tell us what her news is before you start bringing everyone down."

In his defense, he said, "I don't want this perfect meal ruined and her moving away would ruin it."

Jason stated, "We all know how you would feel about Lexi moving away."

"It's just that North Carolina is so far away. We would never see her."

Lexi's mom said sarcastically, "What's the difference between North Carolina and here, we hardly see her as it is."

Noticing the mounting tension, Janie interrupted, "Why don't we let Lexi tell us what her news is."

Lexi looked at her sister-in-law and mouthed, "Thank you."

Janie gave her a thumbs up. Jason looked at his sister and said, "Okay, enough of this. What is this big news you have to tell us?"

Lexi took a deep breath to calm herself, "I'm pregnant."

"Pregnant?"

Everyone except for Jason jumped up, and cheered and shouted, "Congratulations."

"Are you sure?" Jason asked in a condescending tone. "You may be just getting fat."

"Jason, drop it," chastised his wife.

Lexi's mom clapped excitedly, "Oh, I am so excited. Why isn't Bennett here to tell us with you? This is just the best news ever. Now, you and Bennett have to get back together."

"No, Mom, Bennett and I are not getting back together."

Jason had a blank look on his face and asked, "Why? Isn't he the father?" Jason gave Lexi a stern look, and asked, "And if Bennett isn't the father, then just who is responsible?"

Their mom scolded him, "Jason, of all the questions to ask. Of course it's Bennett's."

"Sorry, sorry, sorry." Jason was obviously chagrined. "That was a stupid question to ask. It's just...It seems to me that if they are having a baby, they would want to make this marriage work."

Janie gave him a stern look, "As if. Lexi doesn't have to be married to have this baby."

"Well, how did this happen, then?" Jason asked. "Bennett never seemed to be interested in having kids, and now she's pregnant."

Janie rolled her eyes and pointed a finger at him, "Boy, you should be ashamed of yourself. And as far as how this happened, you should know. We have two kids together."

Waving his hands in the air, "That's not what I meant. I meant why did she get pregnant if their marriage was in trouble?"

Lexi glared at her brother, "It's not like I planned this. And as far as Bennett is concerned, he wants nothing to do with this child." Looking at her family, she informed them, "So, I don't want to hear another word about Bennett."

Lexi's mother asked, "What do you mean he doesn't want anything to do with the baby. It is his baby. He should be happy. I think you are just being too hard on the boy."

Lexi's father broke in, "Now, that is enough. We should be happy for Lexi. I'm going to be a grandfather," looking at his wife, "and you're going to be a grandmother, again." Lexi's dad walked over to her and put his hand on her shoulders, "We will be here for you. If you need anything, anything at all, just let us know." He gave his daughter a big hug, "And I can't be happier that I'm going to be a grandfather again. My baby girl is going to have a baby. This has to be the best day ever."

Chapter 19

As Bennett Daigle stared at the house his soon to be ex-wife lived in, he wondered where he had gone wrong. He had what he considered a good life. He may be forty-two, but still looked good for his age. He had started to acquire a small paunch around his midsection, but hitting the gym had almost banished it for good. He still had a full head of hair and could turn a woman's head with just a smile.

Until Lexi found that receipt in the car, he thought he had it all; a wife at home and a mistress on the side. Why had he been so careless to leave that receipt in her car? He did not even remember putting it in there. Typically, he threw them away at the hotel. He slammed his fist on the steering wheel, "Son of a gun!"

As Kyle drove down Lexi's street, he found himself scanning the vehicles parked on both sides. He did a double take when he saw Bennett's Ford Mustang parked across the street from Lexi's house. He wondered what Bennett was doing here.

Instead of parking in front of Lexi's house, Kyle's gut instinct told him to park further away and find out what Bennett wanted. As he walked up to Bennett's car, he noticed that he was just sitting in his car staring at her house, unmoving. Kyle tapped on the driver's side window and startled Bennett. As he rolled down his window, Kyle asked. "Bennett, what are you doing here?"

Shrugging his shoulders, Bennett replied, "I needed to talk to Lexi about the divorce proceedings and she isn't answering my calls."

An uneasy feeling came over Kyle. He just looked at Bennett; something about his story did not sit right. Lexi never mentioned Bennett calling. He had known Bennett long enough to know that the man may not want Lexi, but he also did not want Lexi to see anyone else. "Well, if you want, I can call her for you. She is taking my phone calls."

Shaking his head, Bennett said, "Nah, man, that is okay. I don't want to put you in the middle of this."

Kyle did not believe a word coming out of his friend's mouth. "Look, I am friends with the both of y'all, and I hate to see this divorce get dirty."

Bennett snidely replied, "This divorce would be over with if Lexi just agreed to the terms of the divorce and signed the damn papers. I don't know why she has to be so difficult."

Looking at his friend, Kyle asked, "Did you honestly expect Lexi to agree to pay you alimony? Come on man, even I know Lexi won't agree to that."

"She talked to you about the divorce."

Shrugging his shoulders, Kyle explained, "Well, we are all friends. She needed someone to talk to."

Aggravated that Lexi was talking to Kyle, Bennett started his car and revved the engine before speeding away. Kyle watched to make sure that Bennett did not double back. As he walked up to Lexi's house, he debated whether or not to tell her that Bennett was sitting out front of her house. He hated to alarm her, especially in her condition, but she may need to keep her guard up just in case this turned out to be a problem.

- -

Lexi opened the door wearing paint-splattered jeans, an old T-shirt and her hair in a ponytail. "Oh, I didn't even realize what time it was. I was painting one of the spare bedrooms. I still can't decide what to do with the nursery."

Kyle slid his hand over the nape of her neck and gave her a hello kiss. She wrapped her arms around his neck and deepened the kiss. He told her, "Hmm, I think you look sexy. So sexy that I could go for a taste of dessert before we cook."

She laughed as she swatted playfully at his arm, "Nope, you have to feed me first."

As she watched him putter around the kitchen, she realized she could get used to this. She found it stimulating to watch him cook.

He had insisted on cooking dinner for her, entirely by himself. As she watched him move around the kitchen with complete ease, she took another sip out of her virgin Bloody Mary and moaned in delight as the zingy concoction tantalized her tongue. Even without the alcohol, it wasn't lacking in flavor. He went all out preparing this Bloody Mary for her, even garnishing the drink with a jumbo boiled shrimp, pickled okra, pickled green beans, celery, and garlic stuffed olives.

After putting the steaks to marinade, he scrubbed and prepared the fingerling potatoes for roasting. As he chopped the vegetables for a salad, she asked, "Are you sure you don't need any help?"

"No, I just want you to sit back and relax."

As he cooked, their conversation flowed smoothly. If only Lexi could stop her mind from drifting back to the kiss. She wondered if he intended to spend the night.

As Kyle started the grill, he asked, "How do you like your steak?"

Just the thought of eating a grilled steak made her mouth water, "Medium rare, please. I am one of those who likes to let the potatoes catch the juices while I enjoy a steak."

"A woman after my own heart. I hate cooking a steak to well done. It is sacrilege to cook a steak until the entire flavor is gone."

While he grilled the steaks, Lexi set the table with several candles. Up above, she watched the sky streak with pink and violet hues as the sun set. She had been slowly working in the yard, and it was taking shape. The other day she discovered what once was a rose garden in the back.   After she cleared out the weeds, the roses started to thrive.

Kyle walked up behind her, putting his arms around her. "The steaks are almost done."

She leaned against him, enjoying the feel of his body next to hers. "You are spoiling me. I can't remember the last time I had a grilled steak, other than in a restaurant."

"I love to grill." Snuggling closer to her, he whispered, "Especially when I have a lovely view."

She looked up at him, "I don't think you are looking at the view."

"Oh yes I am, a perfect view."

She laughed, wishing she could be as relaxed as him; although, he had such an easy going attitude. She needed to have lists and everything organized in her life. Being here with him like this, she wished that they were more than just friends with benefits; however, the benefits were very pleasurable.

If she had known sex with him would be this good, she would have approached him long before meeting Bennett. As her mind drifted back to Bennett, she found herself comparing the two men. Kyle was confident without being arrogant where Bennett was always overly arrogant in everything he did. Kyle never once acted like he was God's gift to women, but Bennett had always acted like he was God's gift to women.

Even taking tonight into consideration, Bennett would never wait on her, whereas Kyle had been nothing but charming and attentive. Lately, Bennett's behavior had been rather unpredictable. Just the other day, she swore Bennett was following her.

Kissing her on the cheek, he reluctantly pulled away, "I need to pull off the steaks so that we can eat."

After he had flipped the steaks onto the plate, they headed back inside. As he served them, she told him, "You know, if you ever wanted to stop running the fishing charters you could run a restaurant."

Holding her chair out for her, he laughed, "I considered it, but there is too much competition out there for restaurants. To be successful here, you need something entirely different."

As she took a bite of her steak, she moaned in delight, "With steaks like this, you would run the others out of business. This is the best steak I have ever had." Taking another bite, she confessed, "I am trying to cook more. When I was married, I attempted to cook some, but it was easier to call the restaurant at the hotel and have them prepare a meal. Now with a baby on the way, I would rather learn how to make us nutritious meals and not depend on the chef at the hotel to feed us. I have to admit though, that it is easier to grab takeout, but it is nowhere near as good as this."

Kyle nodded his head in understanding, "I hate going to a restaurant or bar by myself, but I would rather dine alone instead of prying a woman's claw out of me. It didn't take me long to learn how to cook; it is much easier to eat alone instead of having to hide from the desperate women."

Laughing, Lexi teased him, "Oh, I am sure you enjoy the attention the women give you. You probably lap it up."

"After a while, all of their faces blend into one." He left out that their faces seemed to meld into hers.

"Well, if you had cooked like this for any of those women, I am surprised they let you out of their sights."

"I have never cooked for another woman."

She looked at him, unsure of how to respond to that comment. "Seriously? I am surprised. Cooking like this for a woman would be a sure fire way to grab her hook, line, and sinker."

"Good grief, no. The last thing I want is to marry a woman who has been waiting to sink her claws into me."

"Well then, I guess I should be flattered." She wondered if he had any desire to get married.

Kyle went quiet for a moment, "I have to tell you something, but I don't want you to panic."

Looking at him curiously, she asked, "What is it?"

"Bennett was sitting outside of your house."

"Wait? What? Bennett was out front, sitting in his car?"

Shrugging his shoulders, he explained, "Somehow he figured out where you live. He mentioned you were avoiding his calls, but when I told him to use my phone, he backed off."

She was dumbfounded as to why Bennett was even sitting outside of her house, but it made her uneasy. Now, she wondered if he had followed her the other night. "I don't understand why he would sit out front of the house? Why is he worried about what I am doing? He cheated on me. He wanted a divorce."

"I'm not sure why he was out front, but he was there. He seemed surprised to see me, but he didn't have a good reason to be here."

As she picked up her glass, she noticed her hands were shaking. "It doesn't make any sense."

"I wasn't sure whether or not I should even tell you, but, in the end, I realized you needed to know."

"No, you are right; I needed to know. He has been rather cruel lately when he talks to me, but I figured he wanted to put me down." He started demeaning her after she refused to sign the divorce settlement. She refused to pay him alimony, and any debt he incurred while dating his mistress.

Still, the thought of Bennett sitting outside of her house watching her was unsettling. She liked this house for the privacy it offered. It was a quiet neighborhood, and her neighbors were not right on top of her. She had been so focused on her own little world, she never bothered to look out in the front. How many other times had Bennett been out there watching her? Had he been keeping track of her at the hotel, too? Why?

Kyle must have sensed her anxiety because he came over and took her hands in his and helped her stand up. He wrapped her into his arms. Without speaking, he just held her. This was what she needed more than a lover, someone to comfort her, and show her that they were there for her.

Placing her arms around his waist, she nestled her face into his chest and let his embrace wash her fears away for a short period of time. It felt good being held in his arms, so very right.

He took his finger and tipped her head back. Slowly, his head lowered to meet hers. The kiss was filled with give and take.

After he had devoured her mouth, he whispered in her ear, "Dessert has always been my favorite part of the meal."

- - - - - - - - ● - - - - - - - -

Kyle held Lexi close to his body. This beautiful woman had found a place in his heart and not just as a friend.

Being here with her felt so right in every possible way. He wanted to be by her side day and night.

His hands caressed her growing stomach. For a moment, he thought he felt the baby flutter against his hand. He could not remember the last time he was this happy.

He did not like that she was going through this alone. If this was his child, he would be there. It still surprised him how uncaring Bennett was being.

He could offer moral support, but when it came to parenthood and all that it entailed, she was alone.

Chapter 20

Lexi was cooking breakfast when her phone rang. She groaned when she saw that it was Bennett. It had been three weeks since she heard from him, and she was not in the mood to deal with him this morning. "What do you need Bennett?"

"When are going to call your lawyer and get this divorce settlement worked out?"

"I will see what happens today, but I can't promise you I will get a chance to call my attorney."

Bennett sighed, "I need to get this wrapped up. The bills are piling up. I don't understand why you didn't stay in the house and take over that note. April isn't happy living there; she wants something that we purchased together."

"That sounds like a personal problem to me." Lexi could not believe she had wasted these past few years on a self-absorbed, arrogant man, who would rather her terminate this pregnancy than accept the child. How could she have been so blind to his character flaws?

"I already listed the house, but the agent stated that with the housing market the way it is, it may be a while before it sells. I'm not sure how I am going to pay you your half."

An uneasy feeling came over her that Bennett was outside of her house checking up on her. "Listen, Bennett, I don't care about your financial problems. You made this choice when you decided to dip your wick somewhere else. You wanted the divorce, so you need to work out your financial problems, not me."

As he abruptly ended the call, she peeked out the window, and a shiver of fear ran down her spine. Sure enough, Bennett was sitting in his car across the street from her house. She wondered why he was watching her house.

Where was April and why the sudden interest in her? Was he checking to make sure she was alone? Was he hoping to catch her with another man to use as leverage in the divorce proceedings? Did he not realize she had enough evidence that he had been cheating on her for some time now? She suspected that he'd screwed more than just April. April was a fool if she believed he would remain faithful to her.

As Lexi continued to look out the window, she saw her best friend, Christi, pull up. Forgetting about Bennett, she rushed out the door to welcome her. As soon as Christi got out of her car, the two women were hugging, "I am so happy to see you. What are you doing here?"

"I had a meeting in Springport and wanted to see your new house. And, of course, the new you." Stopping to look around the exterior of the house, she exclaimed, "The house is charming. With some work, it will be perfect."

"I know. I can see myself living here for a long time."

As Christi walked through the interior of the house, she came over and hugged her friend again. "I love this house. It is adorable and just so you."

"I thought that I loved the other house because it was what Bennett wanted, but now, I see that our taste in houses is entirely different."

"I still can't believe you kicked that miserable SOB out of the house." Looking at Lexi's surprised face, she went on, "Oh, come on, you know I never liked the man. I put up with him because he was your husband, and you seemed to be happily married. Although, honestly, I never thought he would be able to keep that snake in his pants."

Lexi laughed at her friend as they walked into the living room, "Well, I guess you were right about that. He won't be able to keep his hands to himself for long with this new woman either. I believe he screwed more women than just April."

"You poor thing, but I wouldn't doubt it." Leaning in closer to her friend, she asked, "I hope you had yourself tested for any diseases that he may have passed on to you."

"You better believe it, sista girl. As soon as I found out." Dropping her voice, she informed her friend, "I am pregnant."

Christi's mouth dropped, "Oh, my...What! Are you serious?" Looking her friend over once more, she asked, "Is that why you have sounded so cheerful lately or did you find someone to make you feel like a woman should?"

Blushing Lexi replied, "Maybe a little of both."

"Girl, you have to tell me all the dirty little details. Don't you dare hold anything back. So, do I know who is putting a smile on your face?"

"It is Kyle DuPont."

Christi's eyes lit up, "What? No way! I thought you two were best of friends growing up. Oh wait, were you doing the horizontal mambo with him back then?"

"No, we weren't. Just lately, we have become friends with benefits."

Christi looked at her suspiciously, "Hmm, you aren't telling me something. That smile you are sporting looks like a woman who is getting some really good loving."

"It isn't good, it is mind-blowing. I have never had an orgasm like those with Kyle. Girl, I tell you there are fireworks. Sometimes I think the fire department will have to be called to put out the flames."

"Oh, I definitely need to find me a man like that. Still, I can't believe that you didn't hook up with him when you were younger."

"Honestly, we never did it back then. Now, I wish we had."

Lexi could see the mischief in Christi's eyes, "So, where do you think this relationship is going? Or is it too soon to tell?"

"After everything that happened with Bennett, I'm not interested in a long-term relationship. I am too leery to trust my heart to a man. Besides, it won't be long before the baby is born. Seriously, do you think any man out there wants to take care of another man's baby? You also have to remember that Bennett and Kyle are friends. Kyle is the one who introduced me to Bennett. I don't think he would be too comfortable raising Bennett's child."

"Yeah, but he has no problems doing the nasty with Bennett's soon to be ex-wife."

"I asked for this, not him. Kyle is not the marrying type. He prefers to love them and leave them, which is what I need right now. I am not looking for a commitment."

"Okay, I have to know. How is Bennett taking the news about being a father?"

Shrugging her shoulders, Lexi said, "He wants me to terminate the pregnancy or give the baby up for adoption."

Concern filled Christi's voice, "That's crazy."

"Girl the man has been acting crazy lately. He actually expects me to pay for half of HIS bills, and he wants me to pay HIM alimony."

"Oh, hell to the no. I sure hope you didn't agree to any of those terms."

"Are you kidding me!? There is absolutely no way I will agree to continue to pay his way. My attorney has drawn up another settlement agreement, but I am so busy that I haven't had a chance to meet with him. It is crazy busy at the hotel and then there is my pregnancy." Tapping her foot on the ground unconsciously, she confided to her friend, "Bennett followed me home one night. When you drove up, he was out there just staring at the house."

Christi let out a gasp, "What? Seriously? Why?"

"I don't understand why he is behaving this way. I mean, he is the one who wanted a divorce. He informed me that I didn't satisfy him as a wife should. He is the one who found another woman, but lately, he has been sitting in front of the house, just staring at it."

"Have you confronted him?"

Shaking her head, Lexi stated, "No. Kyle did, and he had some lame excuse. I talked to my attorney, and if Bennett continues, we can use it to speed the divorce along. Then maybe he will agree to our terms. If not, we can threaten to go to the police and ask for a restraining order to be filed against him."

"I don't know Lexi. I don't like that he is sitting out there in front of your house. It's creepy."

Lexi shrugged her shoulders, "Maybe he is hoping to catch me with another man."

"I don't understand why Bennett is asking you for alimony. Isn't he loaded?"

"He makes a fairly good salary, but my salary is what we used for the little extra things Bennett liked. Now that he doesn't have my salary, he has to watch what he spends. He doesn't like that, at all. He can't go out to eat all the time, and lord knows, he can't check into a hotel for a little fling. The attorneys advised us to tear up the credit cards until the bills are in order."

Laughing Christi stated, "Ah, so I take it his newest fling doesn't work?"

"She's a cashier. But, according to the receipts I found the other day, he had been paying several of her bills out of my salary. My attorney plans on showing that to Bennett and forcing him to pay me back that money along with what he owes me on the house. At first, I was going to wash my hands of the whole matter, but my attorney reminded me that with a baby on the way I need to recoup as much money as I can from him. The birth alone costs nearly twenty thousand dollars."

Letting out a long whistle, Christi said, "Wow, that is a lot of money."

"I know. I am waiting to find out how much the insurance covers."

"Well, I sure hope you are going to get Bennett to pay for half of the birth."

"I haven't decided. Bennett has always said he didn't want children; claims he isn't father material. I still don't understand how this happened. I never once missed a pill, but Dr. Allen said it sometimes happens. He also said that some cold medicines render the pill useless, and I do take a lot of allergy medicines. That is the only thing I can think of." Running her hand along her stomach Lexi said, "Although, I wouldn't change any of it. I am thrilled to death to be having a baby, even if Bennett is the father."

Christi came over and gave her another hug, "I will always be here for you. If you need anything, just ask. What about your parents? Have you told them?"

"They are excited. Mom honestly believes I should forgive and forget. She is desperately trying to convince me to get back together with him."

"What? Did you tell her there is no way you would take that two-timing snake in the grass back?"

Laughing Lexi admitted, "My words were a little harsher than yours, but yes, I told her in no uncertain terms that I will not take Bennett back."

- - - - - - - ● - - - - - - - -

After Christi had left, Lexi went into the kitchen and checked the ingredients on the recipe to be sure she had everything. The recipe didn't appear too complicated.

While she read the directions once again, she began to doubt that she would be able to do this. As she put the sauce to simmer, her doorbell rang. She greeted Kyle and jokingly asked, "Did my kitchen call you out of desperation?"

As soon as Kyle walked inside, the aroma of something cooking greeted him. "Hmm, no it didn't, but by the smell of it, I would say that you are cooking something with oregano and tomatoes. Could it be spaghetti?"

"You are close, but no cigar. I am trying my hand at making lasagna."

"I'm impressed. I love homemade lasagna."

"Good, then you can make sure I am cooking it right. The recipe says to boil the lasagna noodles, but the package says to place them in the pan raw."

"No, you want to make sure you cook them beforehand or it will take longer to cook in the oven. On top of that, the noodles tend to be tougher if you don't cook them ahead of time." Walking over to the sink, he washed his hands before filling a pot with water, "You don't boil them all the way, just al dente."

"See, you arrived in the nick of time. As usual, you are my savior. I would have placed everything in the pan and waited for the blasted thing to finish."

Cooking side by side with Kyle was very domestic, and she was beginning to doubt her true motives. She kept telling herself that they were just friends with benefits, but sometimes when he looked at her, it felt as if it could be something more. She had to keep her heart closely guarded; falling in love with him was the last thing she needed.

As he watched her measure out the olive oil, herbs, and vinegar for the salad dressing, he encouraged her, "And you said that you couldn't cook. You are doing a pretty good job of it."

"Well, I guess this practicing to cook is helping. Thankfully, there are a lot of detailed recipes online. Besides, with the way this baby likes to eat, it is a good thing I am starting to cook, or I would go broke eating out."

She opened the refrigerator and pointed to the chocolate cake, "Although, I did cheat and stop by the bakery to pick up a cake. It is my favorite, too. Chocolate cake layered with white chocolate mousse and topped with a rich chocolate ganache."

As she turned back to toss the salad, she admitted, "I am starting to love cooking though. It is fun to shop for the ingredients."

When the timer for the lasagna went off, Kyle opened the oven door as the aroma of the lasagna wafted out. As he pulled the hot bubbling pan out, she gathered the plates and forks. He carried the lasagna over to the dining room table, and she set the plates, forks, and napkins on the table. Next, she gathered the salad while he poured them each a glass of water.

Once seated at the table, he picked up his fork and took a bite out of the lasagna, "This is delicious."

"Thank you." She took a small bite of the lasagna, fearing that he was just being nice. "Oh, my goodness. This is better than I thought it would turn out."

Chapter 21

Lexi scanned the restaurant and bar for Kyle. She told him that she would meet him here tonight. Now, as she searched the crowded area, she wished she had told him to wait for her outside. She grew uncomfortable as several men noticed her; their eyes watched her every move. But she had no desire to meet any of them. She had no intentions of becoming involved with a man.

She got worried when she did not see Kyle. Perhaps she'd heard him wrong. She searched her purse for her cell phone. As soon as she found it, a voice called out from behind her, "I hope you weren't waiting long?"

"You scared me. I thought perhaps I had heard you wrong."

He shook his head, "I was tied up in a meeting. I tried to call you, but your phone went straight to voicemail."

She looked at her phone and groaned, "It must have died on the way over here."

As they made their way to the table, she looked him over through veiled eyes. He was exceptionally handsome tonight in his khakis and navy blue shirt. Her eyes gravitated to his impressive biceps. And his pants rode low on his lean hips and hugged his muscular body.

She could not understand why this man was still single. He was definitely what women went for in a man. "I hope you are hungry."

She nodded at him, "Are you kidding!? As usual, I am starving."

The restaurant's dim lights along with the sultry jazz music playing in the background made for a cozy, romantic setting; yet, both of them had to remind themselves that this was not a date. This was merely two good friends meeting for supper. After all, they were best friends.

As their waitress placed a basket of fresh bread on the table, she asked them, "Would either of you care for a drink from the bar?"

Lexi informed her, "I would like a glass of sweet tea."

Kyle told the waitress, "I would like water with a lemon wedge, please."

After the waitress had left to get their drinks, Lexi informed Kyle, "You could have ordered a drink. I don't mind."

"Nonsense. I am fine with water."

As the waitress set down their drinks, she told them, "Our special tonight is a Bon Temp Poulet. The chef takes a grilled, marinated chicken breast and serves it over a bed of delicious fresh spinach Rockefeller topped with a creamy pesto sauce and baby shrimp. We are also offering for an appetizer a Seafood Au Gratin. The chef prepares shrimp and crabmeat in a lustrous and velvety, creamy cheese sauce, and served over slices of French bread."

Lexi looked over at Kyle and informed him, "Well, I don't know about you, but the special sounds wonderful. I would like that."

Kyle told the waitress, "We would like to start off with the Seafood Au Gratin and two specials also, please.

As they waited for their food, Lexi found herself unable to take her eyes off of Kyle tonight. She was starting to enjoy the attention he lavished on her. Bennett never once treated her this special. If she did not reel herself in, she would find her heart melting as she fell in love with this man.

She tore her gaze away from Kyle as the waitress placed the Seafood Au Gratin on the table. No sooner than they finished their appetizer; the waitress placed their entrees in front of them. She moaned in ecstasy as she ate her food. Her taste buds came to life with each bite. "The food is to die for. It is well worth the wait."

"The food is excellent."

Kyle watched Lexi from across the table. When she gave him one of her killer grins that showed off her dimples, he struggled to find his composure as his heart beat a little faster. Her smile melted away his reserve. It came from deep within herself. Every day that he was near her, he found it harder and harder to fight his love for her. If he wanted to walk away from her tonight, he needed to picture her as a friend and nothing more.

Chapter 22

Lexi woke up drenched in sweat. She tried to shake the last of the dream out of her mind. This last dream about Kyle had been steamier than her previous dreams.

- - - - - ● ● ● ● ● ● ● ● ● ● ● ● - - - -

As she turned on the shower, she told herself to snap out of it. While these last couple of months had been heavenly, Kyle would never be interested in a permanent relationship with her. He could have any woman he wanted and did not want scraps left over from his friend. Besides, no man wanted to get involved with a woman who was carrying another man's child. She had to face the fact that she would die a lonely woman who only had her child to love her.

As if sensing she was thinking about him, her phone rang, "Morning."

A shiver ran through her at the sound of his voice. "Morning. What are you doing up this early?"

"How would you like to go fishing?"

She laughed, "Seriously?   I haven't been fishing in years."

"Well, get dressed. I will be there shortly."

She reminded him, "You do know that you can find a very willing woman who would love to keep you company."

"I am asking a very willing woman to go fishing with me. Besides, I don't have to worry about you wanting a marriage certificate and diamond ring."

- - - - - ● ● ● - - - - - -

Before leaving his house, Kyle made sure he did not forget to bring the picnic basket Maria, his housekeeper, had packed. Today, he planned to take his newest fishing boat out before any customers had a chance to use it. This allowed him the opportunity to see how the new captain handled the boat. He had been ecstatic when the broker called him about the thirty-foot Osprey Pilothouse Long Cabin. Since Osprey fishing boats were uncommon here, the deal was too good to pass up.

It was an unbeatable quality for an ultimate sport fishing boat. This particular boat came with twin diesels with a 450-mile cruising range. The reviews stated that the performance of this boat was unmatched by its competition. When they took it out on the water, he had to admit that it was a smooth ride for a deep V cruiser. What made it perfect for him was it slept six people. The Pilothouse had a 360-degree visibility, full walk around deck, electric controls, and even a stand-up head with shower. The seventy-six square foot aft deck gave the customers plenty of room to reel in the largest catch of the day.

As he placed the basket in the trunk of his car, he peeked inside to see what Maria had put together. She packed Brie and crackers as well as the makings for a virgin Bloody Mary along with the glasses. There was also an antipasto plate with various olives along with smoked turkey, Gouda cheese, and her famous fig spread for her homemade croissant rolls. His mouth was already watering. Maria even packed a few chocolate filled croissants and a fantastic dessert assortment for them to nibble on. Even his mom had never packed anything as extravagant as this for him when he went fishing as a kid.

On the drive to Lexi's house, he wondered if she would ever see him as more than a friend. They grew up together. They climbed trees together, rode bikes and got into all kinds of trouble together. He was the one who introduced her to Bennett. When they all hung out together, she sometimes felt like a third wheel, that was until she and Bennett became an item.

Knocking on the door, he anxiously waited for her to answer. "Good morning. I hope you're ready to catch some fish."

Lexi laughed, "I hope you are patient with me. I don't remember the last time I went fishing, and I sure don't remember the last time I was on a boat."

"No worries, I will be patient with you. So, what sort of payment are we looking at if I help you catch a few fish? I have a few suggestions if you need some ideas."

"Down boy. I know what you want."

He gave her a wicked grin as he put his hand on his heart, "I am as innocent as a schoolboy. Besides, I was going to say that you had to cook supper one night in return for me taking you fishing today."

She laughed at his remark, "Even as a schoolboy you weren't innocent. I seem to recall all sorts of stunts that you came up with that constantly landed us in trouble."

"What? That is not true! I was curious is all."

On the drive, they continued their talk. Before either knew it, they were at the dock. The trip seemed to be faster than normal.

Anxious to see what she thought of his newest boat, he helped her onto the deck. Lexi looked around, and stated, "I'm impressed. This is much nicer than I imagined. The pictures of the boat you messaged me did it no justice."

"You are sworn to secrecy about the spot I am taking you. My newest captain swears that it is the best spot on the river. I am anxious to find out how good this fishing hole is. Supposedly, it is the best because a small bayou meets the Mississippi River."

She looked up at him with mischief in her eyes, "I swear my lips are sealed about your secret location. My dad has a few spots like that and he swore me to secrecy when he took me fishing. Mom always hated when he would take me fishing, too. She didn't think it was proper for ladies to go fishing, but I loved it. That was our special time together. Jason never cared to fish. He spent most of his time chasing girls and playing sports."

As the captain drove the boat to the fishing spot, Kyle busied himself setting up their poles. Lexi looked over everything he had brought with him, and told him, "I sure don't remember you being a boy scout when we were young."

"I wanted to be prepared in case you got hungry or perhaps bored from watching me bring in all the fish."

She laughed at this comment. "You honestly think that you will catch that many more fish than me."

"Ah, but I have a secret weapon. An old fisherman told me the secret on how to catch more fish than any other boat on the water."

Once they were ready to bait the hooks, he opened up the bait, and the smell nearly knocked her out. Wrinkling her nose, she took the neck of her shirt and covered her nose and mouth, as she mumbled, "What is in there?" She swore that she could feel herself turning green from the smell.

"It is a mixture of chicken liver and squid."

"Well, it smells awful."

He laughed so hard at the face she made that he had actual tears coming out of his eyes. "I guess that means I have to put it on the hook for you."

After an hour of fishing, Lexi admitted defeat. With her hands in the air, she surrendered, "Okay, I don't know how you do it, but there is no way I will catch up. I say we wash up and eat. I already saw what is packed in the basket and can't wait to dive in."

"Yeah, Maria packed a variety of things that she thought you would like."

"You could have lied and taken the credit."

"Nah, that wouldn't have been right. Besides, you have been lied to enough."

"Ain't that the truth!"

Chapter 23

Bennett stared at Lexi's front door and scowled. He knew she was at work, and this may be the only time he could do this. There had to be something in there that he could use as leverage in this divorce. He looked at his watch and realized that if he wanted to do this, it was now or never.

- - - - - • • • ● • • • • - - - -

When Lexi arrived home earlier than usual that evening she saw two police cruisers parked out front of her house, her heart skipped a beat. Her dread increased when she saw a police officer standing in her front yard, talking on the radio. Several neighbors that she had not even met yet were clustered together on the street.

Great introduction to the neighborhood, she thought as she got out of her car. "Is there a problem here officer?" She asked as she walked towards him.

The officer tipped his hat, "Ma'am, is this your house?"

"Yes, it is. Has something happened?"

"Your neighbor called in to say that you possibly had an intruder."

Lexi looked at him dumbfounded. "I'm sorry, sir, but someone broke into my house?"

He nodded his head, "It appears so. I need you to wait outside until we make sure that the house is clear. We have two officers inside right now."

Lexi looked at him, puzzled, "But how did they get inside?"

"I'm sorry to tell you this, but your back door appeared to have been jimmied open."

A shiver of fear snaked down Lexi's spine. Why would someone want to break into her house? A voice crackled over the officer's radio, and he informed Lexi, "The intruder is still inside and has been apprehended. They are bringing him out now. Would you rather wait in your car?"

Shaking her head, she asked, "What is going to happen to him?"

"They will be taking him downtown. While he is being booked, I will walk through the house with you, to ensure that everything is as it should be."

Lexi wondered if this was a random break and enter, or did this neighborhood have problems she did not know about. As she stood in the front yard, she watched as two more officers appeared with a man in handcuffs. Was that… "Wait a minute, I think that's my ex-husband."

Not thinking clearly, and honestly not caring, she rushed toward them. It was Bennett with his hands cuffed behind his back.

Lexi looked at him, "You broke into my house?" Anger bubbled up inside her. "Why?"

The officer to the right of Bennett asked, "You know this man?"

"Unfortunately, I do. He is my soon to be ex-husband." Furious at Bennett, "We are separated, and waiting for the divorce to be finalized," she informed the police officers.

The police officers secured Bennett in the back seat of one of the cruisers, and walked back to where Lexi was standing. The police officer informed Lexi, "We're going to take him downtown, so we can get him processed. Officer Donaldson is going to stay here and go through the house with you."

Lexi was still seething, but informed the officer, "Yes, sir, I understand."

Officer Donaldson looked at Lexi, "So the divorce is not finalized?"

Lexi ruefully shook her head, "Not yet."

One of the other police officers told Lexi, "He will be arrested. He does not live here, and his name is not on the lease. He will be charged with breaking and entering."

A hint of a smile twitched on Lexi's face, "Do what you need to do officer. I will get in touch with my landlord and let him know that Bennett damaged the back door."

The officer informed Lexi, "The landlord will likely also charge him with destruction of personal property."

Lexi dreaded involving her new landlord. He was a sweet, elderly man, who did not need this hassle in his life.

Officer Donaldson told Lexi, "Let's go inside so that you can go through the place. He probably wasn't in there for long, but I'd like to make sure nothing is missing."

"Of course, yes sir."

They spent nearly half an hour going through the house, making sure the windows were locked and nothing was missing.

"I'm not sure why he broke in. We recently separated our household belongings. He kept the house and the furniture that was inside it."

"Perhaps he was looking for some jewelry? Rings?"

"I gave those to Bennett in the divorce settlement. I don't know why he would be here."

"I need to get back to the precinct. Here's my card with the case number. Please give me a call if you notice anything missing or have any concerns."

"Thank you, I appreciate all the help."

"Things like this can be unnerving. You may want to have a friend or family member come stay with you for a bit."

"Thank you for the recommendation. With Bennett arrested, I'm sure I'll be fine."

As Officer Donaldson left, he said, "Take care."

Lexi shut the door, locked it, and plopped on the couch. Tears of frustration flowed down her cheeks. Eye for an eye, Bennett Daigle.

Chapter 24

Lexi grimaced as she listened to the voice mail. "Lexi dear, it's mom. It's seven o'clock in the morning, why aren't you answering your phone? Call me."

Lexi had to shake her head. Her mom knew that her day started early, yet she insisted on calling every day when she was in her morning meeting. She would have to call her back later, after things had calmed down at the hotel.

Only, before Lexi could continue her day, her mom breezed into her office, without knocking. "Lexi, darling, there you are. I was so worried about you when you didn't return my call."

Lexi held back any sarcastic comments, "Mom, I have meetings every morning at seven. I just got into my office, and haven't had a chance to call you back." She said as she walked over and shut her office door. No reason for everyone to hear the coming lecture.

"Work, work, work. That's all you think about. Please tell me you have finally come to your senses and are getting back with Bennett."

In a rather forceful tone, "Mother. I am not getting back together with Bennett."

"Why not?" Her mother asked. "It would make me so happy if you did."

Lexi walked over and gave her mom a reassuring hug, "Mom, I know you are upset about the divorce. But it is going to happen. Bennett and I are through. I'm sorry, but that's the way it is. We will not be getting back together."

"This whole thing is just absurd. Maybe if you saw a therapist you can work things out."

The words came out terser than she wanted. "Mom, my marriage is over, and it is time for you to accept it, please."

Sadly, she said, "I will try."

- - - - - - - - ● ● ● ● - - - -

On the drive home from the hotel, Lexi found herself looking in her rearview mirror. She constantly worried that Bennett was following her every move lately.

She reflected on all the changes in her life these last few months. With so many sudden changes it was nearly impossible to keep up with everything.

This week alone had been so busy that she had not been able to keep up with all of her appointments. She met with the attorney, her doctor, and had to deal with the craziness going on with the hotel.

Currently, she was waiting to see how Bennett took the changes her attorney and she made to the divorce settlement. She suspected that it would not go over well.   However, she hoped by not going after his investments, he would sign the divorce settlement. She didn't want anything of his. However, her lawyer insisted that she at least seek reimbursement of the funds he used that belonged to her on the mistress, along with a fifty percent split of the proceeds of the house. She refused to pay him alimony and in turn, she would not ask him for any either. As far as child support, she requested that it not be brought up yet. She would rather see how well this current settlement went.

As she neared her house, her heart dropped. Almost directly in front of her house was Bennett's car. She swallowed down the lump caught in her throat. She prayed that he was not here to confront her about the divorce settlement. The last thing she wanted was a personal confrontation with him. Especially after the break in fiasco.

As soon as Bennett saw her pulling up, he stepped out of his car. Before she could even get out of the car, he was hollering, "Why haven't you answered any of my phone calls today?"

"I have been in and out of meetings all day Bennett. Besides, I am no longer your wife and no longer have to answer to you."

"That is complete bullshit. The divorce is still not final, so technically, you are still my wife."

She could strangle him right now. His vehement words had her stunned. "Seriously, Bennett. You never seemed to be concerned about our marriage when you were screwing another woman, now did you?"

Tired of dealing with him, she turned her back to him and started walking towards her front door. She was surprised when he grabbed her arm and whipped her around to face him. As his grasp on her forearm strengthened, he went on to say, "I wasn't done talking yet."

Shaking her arm free, "Well, I am DONE talking to you. If you have anything else to say to me, go through my attorney Bennett. That is, unless you want me to call the police to come pick you up. Again."

Once safely inside of her house, she flipped the deadbolt shut and leaned against the door for support. He had never acted like this before; never grabbed her like that. What was wrong with him?

Suddenly, her stomach felt queasy. Covering her mouth, she ran to the bathroom. After a few minutes, she hauled herself to her feet and splashed cold water on her face. While brushing her teeth, she caught a glimpse of herself in the mirror and was grateful that she had not become sick in front of him. The last thing she needed was him asking what was wrong with her.

Even now, she still looked like death warmed over. She had hoped the morning sickness part was over, but it seemed like it could happen at any time of the day, not just mornings. She told herself that it could be from the stress of dealing with Bennett that caused her stomach to start rolling.

In the kitchen, she fixed herself a piece of dry toast and a cup of tea. Trying to ignore the lightheadedness, she snuggled into the couch and pulled an afghan over her knees. She nibbled on a corner of the toast as she thought about how angry Bennett had been towards her. Where was this anger coming from? She was the victim in all of this; yet, he was acting like she was the one betraying him.

Keeping her breathing shallow, she swallowed hard as the bile started to rise in her throat again. Thinking of Bennett did neither her nor the baby any good. She should take better care of herself and eat on a more regular basis.

When she heard her doorbell ring, she jumped. She was afraid to see who it was, just in case it was Bennett coming back to torture her some more. She looked through the peephole and smiled when she saw Kyle there. He was holding a large bouquet of white roses with Asiatic lilies and pink tea roses.

"This is a surprise."

He kissed her on the cheek and handed her the flowers. "Bennett called and asked if I could please talk some sense into his deranged wife. I assumed if he was calling me, then he must have given you a hell of a day already."

She opened the door wider for him, "That man is the devil reincarnate. He was in such a mood." Taking the flowers from him, "But, thank you for the flowers. These are beautiful".

He asked her, "Let me take you out to supper, please?"

"I don't know. I have felt like crap ever since my run in with Bennett, and I am not dressed to go out."

Pushing her towards her bedroom, he said, "Go get dressed. Besides, you still need to eat, don't you?"

"I guess."

After she had freshened up, he escorted her outside and opened the car door for her. She slipped into the passenger seat of the Range Rover. "This SUV is growing on me. After all, I have to trade my car in on something more practical."

He grinned, "Yeah, it may be difficult putting a baby seat in the back seat of your car."

She chuckled as she ran her hands along the soft leather interior. "I know. Every time I get into the car, I try to picture myself getting in and out with a car seat. It won't be a pleasant experience on a daily basis."

"I will take you car shopping one day. I am a car fanatic and can spend the day looking at the new cars coming out."

"So, where are you planning on taking me out for supper?"

"Since you like Italian food so much, I thought we would go get a pizza at That's Amore."

She excitedly said, "That is one of my favorite restaurants."

He admitted, "I remember. We used to go there all the time to get their Mona Lisa Pizza. I wasn't sure if it was still your favorite though. As much as I love Angelo's, you can't beat the lasagna or pizza at That's Amore."

The ride to the restaurant was quiet as Lexi thought about the things she did before Bennett. "It has probably been five years since I have been there to tell you the truth. I dragged Bennett there a few times, but it wasn't his cup of tea. Come to think of it, I don't think he eats pizza."

She laid her head back against the headrest, let the luxury of the car relax her, and took in the beautiful night. As they crossed over the Mississippi River Bridge, she watched as the moonlight danced across the languid waves. She could get lost in the slow, steady waves as they caressed the bank. Sighing, she said, "There are times that I wish I lived on the water. It is so peaceful."

"That is why I love doing the fishing charters. I try to ride with the captains and clients as much as possible. I am finding it addicting to be out there on the open water."

She felt the car slow down and realized they were at their destination. "I can already taste the pizza."

He looked over at her, "It is nice going out with you for dinners again. I have missed having you beside me so that we can just talk about nothing important; besides, you look so cute sitting there."

- - - - - - ● ● ● ● - - - - - -

Once seated in the restaurant, he ordered an antipasto platter for an appetizer.

As she looked over the menu, her mouth watered. "Oh my, they have added a few more pizzas since the last time I was here."

"The muffuletta pizza is new. While it is good, I prefer the Carnivore."

She let out a soft chuckle, "If you don't hush, I will order half the menu. The chicken and feta pizza sounds good, too, but I read somewhere that feta isn't good for pregnant women to eat."

"Well, let's order a couple of pizzas. Then, you can have cold pizza for breakfast."

She laughed, "I honestly can't believe just how much you remember about me. There is nothing like cold pizza." Leaning in, she confessed, "It would drive Bennett nuts when I brought home BBQ chicken from Jim Bob's just so that I could have it for breakfast."

"Okay, I admit that I am a little dumbfounded as to why that would drive him nuts?"

"Bennett has this thing about leftovers. He never liked even having them in the house."

They talked and laughed for hours. The night passed by quickly, and before they knew it, the waiter was telling them that they would be closing soon.

Lexi was surprised, "I didn't realize we had been talking so long."

As Kyle escorted her back to his car, he said, "It has been a very pleasant evening. One I don't want to end."

"Thank you for making this night perfect. It is just what I needed to take my mind off the problems I had with Bennett earlier."

He asked, "We are making it a habit to meet for supper, aren't we?"

"I know. As much as I enjoy it, I am probably keeping you from living your own life."

He kissed her hand, "For you, I have no qualms about putting things aside."

She looked up at him, "You should be wining and dining women, having your one night stands, and being a playboy. You should not be trying to keep a lonely, pregnant woman from falling into a pit of self-misery."

She noticed the twinkle in his eyes. "Oh please, you are more interesting than any of the women I have met recently. Besides, just the thought of a date with a single woman sends chills down my spine. A root canal would be more pleasurable."

"That bad, huh? I must say I am not too anxious about entering the dating pool again."

Once at her house, he went around and opened the car door for her. He took her hand in his and escorted her to the front door. He placed a finger under her chin and tilted her face up, bending down and kissing her gently, "Thank you for having supper with me, Lexi."

The gentle kiss shook her to the very center of her being. She looked into his eyes and saw the desire building. She wrapped her arms around him and deepened the kiss. He took the keys from her and unlocked the door, "I am glad that I decided to surprise you tonight."

Lexi watched as he drove away, disappointed that he did not want more than just a kiss.

- - - - - - - - - - - - - - - - - - - -

As Kyle drove away from Lexi's house, it took all of his self-control to keep from turning around, driving back and showing her just how much he wanted her. It was getting harder and harder to keep his hands to himself when he was near her.

He could tell when he arrived at her house earlier that she was not feeling well, and they stayed out later than they should have. If she didn't need her rest, he would have stayed and kept her up most of the night.

Chapter 25

Christi pushed Lexi into her room. "Shake a leg girlie. We have people waiting."

Lexi bit back a moan. While she appreciated the thought, she dreaded attending a party to celebrate her failed marriage. "It's sweet of you to do this for me, but I will probably bring the party down."

"Doll, we are celebrating tonight. When will you realize that your life is better off without him?" Giving her one last shove into the room she said, "Now, get ready. I have a few surprises planned."

Lexi stood at the door and waved her hands in the air, "I've had enough surprises to last me a lifetime, thank you very much. All I want is to settle into a nice quiet routine and wait for my baby to be born."

Christi looked at her friend, "I know Bennett did a number on you. He put you through a horrible ordeal, but please, don't let him keep you down."

"You know, I have often wondered if my marriage would have turned out differently if I hadn't taken the promotion and devoted more time to it. Perhaps I am the reason why the marriage failed. I keep hearing my mother warn me that I would lose Bennett if I didn't get home right away. She always lectured me on what

I should do to be the perfect wife and complained that I spent too much time at work."

Christi waved her finger in the air and shook her head, "That's complete and utter nonsense. Bennett was the reason that your marriage failed. He just couldn't keep it in his pants." Smiling, she added, "Besides, perhaps you can find someone there tonight that will help you work out any kinks you may have."

Lexi gave her friend a dubious look, "Just what did you plan tonight?"

"Girlie, it is time you learned the benefits of rebounding."

"And what makes you think that I haven't rebounded enough with my friends with benefits deal that I have with Kyle?"

Christi looked at her friend and saw the twinkle in her eye, "Oh, my gosh! You have rebounded haven't you?" With silly theatrical dramatics, Christi put the back of her hand to her forehead and said, "How could I have forgotten!"

Lexi laughed, "It's nothing really. I just needed someone to prove to me that I am still desirable."

"And…Is he still helping with great satisfaction?"

"Let's say that I feel better about myself."

"I have to admit he is definitely a man I would consider pursuing a friends with benefits relationship with. Now get in there and doll yourself up. You need to move forward and stop looking at the past." Lexi closed her bedroom door, took a deep breath and leaned against the door for a short moment before walking across the room to get ready for her party.

Once she applied her makeup, she rummaged through the closet and tried to decide what to wear. Most of her clothes were getting too tight, and what did fit her was not made for a "divorce party". As she moved clothes around, she found a slinky deep burgundy wrap dress. It was form fitting at the top, tied at the waist and fell to a full skirt hitting just below the knees. The lustrous fabric was finely cut and flattered her figure. What made it even better was the dress fell in a way that hid her pregnancy.

Before leaving her room, she looked at her reflection in the mirror, turning this way and that way. She had to admit that she looked damn good for a pregnant woman.

Once at Faux Pas, Lexi let out a groan when she found out Christi had not only invited everyone here to celebrate, but also rented a private room. She whispered to her friend, "Please don't tell me that there will be half naked men dancing around here."

"Relax, it's just a party. We are going to celebrate your liberation from that dipstick."

Once the party was going, Lexi found herself getting lost in the crowd. She could actually feel a spike in her energy as the enthusiastic partygoers danced.

The energy around her was contagious. Her pulse moved in sync with the rhythm of the music. As she was enjoying the party, Christi walked up to her. Lexi gave her a big hug, "I admit it, you were right. The party is fantastic." She twirled around the room, taking in the streamers and balloons, "Even the decorations are just perfect."

Before Christi could say another word, Kyle walked up to the two of them, holding up a bag, "Where do we put the gifts?"

Christi pointed to the end of the bar, "You can add it to the collection."

It was not long before the room was booming with music and laughter. Lexi made the rounds, thanking everyone for attending.

Just as Lexi finished welcoming the newest arrival, Kyle walked over to her, "This is a great party. Are you enjoying yourself?"

She nodded her head, "Christi did a fabulous job with it. I wasn't sure at first about a divorce party, but now

I am really enjoying myself." Holding up her drink, she said, "Even if I can only drink ginger ale."

Before Kyle and Lexi could converse further, Christi pulled her over to the bar, "Come on, girlie, it is time to open some gifts."

As Lexi looked over the crowd waiting for her to open the gifts, she suddenly felt very sorry for herself. Repulsion for Bennett and the stress he had put her through seemed to take over her whole being.

Christi handed her the first one, snapping her out of her reverie. Christi held up a glass for a toast, "I want to thank everyone for coming out here to celebrate Lexi's divorce. As most of you know, she would never speak ill of Bennett, but I for one am glad that she is rid of the lying, cheating sack of manure. Here is to Lexi and her new life without her baggage."

Everyone erupted in laughter as Christi finished her toast. She looked back at Lexi and informed her, "The gifts are anonymous and strictly for fun. With that being said, let's get to opening, Lexi."

Lexi read the card before opening the gift, "Welcome to the single world once again." She laughed as she revealed a box of condoms. Subsequent gifts revealed various T-shirts, adult toys, massage oils, and some very slinky lingerie that brought on even more laughter. Lexi could feel her cheeks turn red as she opened the last box. Someone had bought her a vibrator to use. The card read, "It may not please you the same, but at least it doesn't talk back either." Lexi had to brush away the tears falling from her eyes.

By the end of the night, Lexi was exhausted. When Kyle wrapped his arms around her, she almost fell into him, relishing in the warmth of his embrace. He whispered in her ear, "You know you don't need those artificial items to bring you pleasure. I, however, would love to see you in a few of those revealing lingerie pieces."

"Something tells me that one or two of those are from you."

"Who, me? Why would I do that?" Taking her hand in his, he said, "Come on lady, let's get you home."

Being this close to Kyle had her suddenly very aware of him as a man. *"No! You can only see Kyle as a friend. You cannot afford more heartache,"* she told herself.

Chapter 26

All you could see of Lexi's eyes were the perfectly shaded coppers of her eyeshadow. She took a deep breath in as she tried to steady her jittery nerves.

No matter how many times they rearranged the tables and chairs, she could not seem to get it perfect. The bride's mother had called again and added several more guests to the list of people attending the wedding reception tomorrow.

Letting out another curse under her breath, she looked around the large ballroom once more. Being one of the few hotels in Springport with a room capable of holding two hundred or more guests, they stayed busy. However, this was the first time she had problems arranging a party. She did not know if it was because this was a wedding or that she was feeling sorry for herself. Whatever the reason, she needed to get her tuchus in gear, or she would not have anything ready for tomorrow night. Thankfully, the staff had cleaned up after tonight's party, so all she had left to do was arrange the tables. In the morning, the staff could decorate.

Unable to stand anymore, she plopped herself down at one of the tables. Leaning her head back, she took in another deep breath and reminded herself that she could do this. She had done this plenty of times.

Tomorrow would be no different from the other parties she had thrown here. She needed to get a grip on her runaway emotions, especially if she wanted to get back home to relax.

Once again, she closed her eyes and blocked out the frenzied activity taking place in the ballroom. If only she could close her ears to the surrounding noises, maybe she could concentrate. Instead, all she could focus on was the noise of the vacuum cleaners, busboys rushing about and the clattering of dishes.

Pressing her fingers firmly against her temples, she tried to will away the headache building. Just as she was ready to run away and hide, a moment of clarity hit her. She started ordering tables to be moved around. With lightning speed, everything began to take shape. As the last of the tables and chairs were arranged in their correct location, the clock showed midnight. So much for getting to bed at a decent hour, but at least it was done.

- - - - - - - - ● - - - - - - - - - -

The next afternoon, Lexi left the office early to meet up with Kyle at a clothing boutique downtown. As she rounded the corner, she saw him waiting for her. As usual, he looked devilishly handsome, and her heart skipped a beat or two before resuming its natural rhythm. She reminded herself that he was only here to offer some much needed moral support and to give her a second opinion on several outfits.

As soon as he saw her, he smiled. "I hope you haven't been waiting too long."

He gave her a quick kiss, "No, I just got here."

The mere brush of his lips caused a delicious whirlpool of emotions to flutter in her stomach.

While walking down the street, window shopping, one store caught Lexi's attention. She turned to Kyle, "Can you stay here for a moment, please. I want to go inside and take a look?"

When Kyle saw that it was a lingerie store, he pushed her towards the door, "Yes, you are more than welcome to go in there unchaperoned. That is one store I have no desire to visit today."

"You are too funny."

Raising his eyebrows, he teased Lexi, "But I want you to model everything you buy today."

Lexi laughed as she swatted him away. "I promise I won't be long."

Wanting to feel girly and prove to herself that she was still beautiful even though she was pregnant, Lexi splurged and bought herself some new lingerie. There was no law that said a girl had to only wear sexy lingerie for a man.

After they had finished shopping, Kyle asked her, "Do you want to grab a cup of coffee before heading back to work?"

"I took the afternoon off. A cup of coffee and beignets sound perfect."

The coffee shop was quiet when they arrived. Kyle told her, "Sit down, and I will get us our café au lait and beignets."

As she set her packages down, she looked out the window and watched as people passed. Since there were not too many people walking by, she turned her attention to Kyle. The barista was a cute woman who was busy flirting with him. Women gravitated toward him and responded to his sexy good looks with open flirting.

- - - - - - - - - ● - - - - - - - - -

As they finished their beignets and café au lait, Kyle started dreading the end to such a lovely day. "Let's stop by the grocery store and pick up a few things for supper."

Laughing, she told him, "You don't have to cook supper for me."

"I want to. You can take a nap, and I will cook us a nice dinner. We can watch a movie afterward."

"A girl can get used to this kind of treatment."

- - - - - - - - - - ● - - - - - - - - - -

While Lexi took a quick nap, Kyle prepared supper. As he was getting ready to cook the pork chops, he heard her leave her bedroom. She took his breath away standing there in the doorway, "You look refreshed, absolutely stunning."

She blushed at the compliment. After her nap, she had changed into a pair of the jeans and T-shirt that she had bought. Her sexy, form-fitting clothes were no longer comfortable, and there was no hiding her pregnancy any longer.

She pulled up a stool at the bar and apologized, "I didn't mean to sleep that long. I set the alarm for thirty minutes and did not hear it go off. Can I help you with something?"

He shook his head, "I have everything under control; besides, your body was telling you that you needed the rest."

"This is heaven for me. You are spoiling me way too much."

As he cooked supper, she fixed them a fresh pitcher of tea, "Do you want me to open you a bottle of wine?"

"Tea is fine by me. I am easy."

"Well, I know you are easy. Still, you can have a drink even if I can't."

Laughing, he said, "No, really, I am good. Tea is fine."

- - - - - - - ● ● ● ● - - - - -

As Lexi watched him, she wished she were as comfortable with cooking as he was. For a man of his size, she found he moved around the kitchen with complete efficiency and ease. As she watched his fluid movements, she could not take her eyes off his muscles. If she closed her eyes, she could feel those massive arms wrapped around her right now.

As the kitchen filled with the aromas of the food he was cooking, the baby gave her a good kick. "Okay, the baby has confirmed that you can cook for us anytime. If I lived with you, I would probably weigh two hundred pounds."

She watched as he wrapped the thick pork chops in bacon, "Okay, that is a new technique."

"I experimented one night and found that wrapping them in bacon not only gives them a smoked taste without having to light the grill, but it keeps them from drying out."

"Hey, you had me at bacon. I am a sucker for bacon."

The evening passed by quickly. As usual, she found herself not wanting the night to end. She had enjoyed sitting this close to him. Desire for him built inside of her. She found herself wanting one more night in his arms. It may be wrong, but she wanted him to make love to her.

- - - - - - - - - - - - - - - - - -

As Kyle prepared to leave, he looked at the woman he was falling madly in love with. For a moment, he considered telling her how he felt, instead he took her in his arms and pulled her close. Unable to resist kissing her, he took her soft, warm lips in his. The kiss started slowly but quickly progressed with a sense of urgency.

He pulled her closer to his hard body as he moved his tongue over her lips. Embers of desire turned into hot passion. Her head dropped back as his lips left a trail of hot kisses down her neck. His eyes gleamed with his desire. Was she falling in love with him? Was her heart his for the taking?

Chapter 27

Kyle arrived at the Springport Municipal Airport earlier than normal. He had a hangar here at the airport to house his Cessna. It was easier than renting a storage space on the outside.

He had just purchased a small private jet to add to his fleet of transportation, and he wanted to know how to fly that as well. He liked to be prepared for the unexpected. He never wanted to be caught with his guard down regarding any matter.

He was a born aviator. His dad allowed him to fly when he was a teenager, and he was immediately hooked. By the time he turned eighteen, he had his pilot's license. Not long after that, he earned his instrument rated instructor with a multi-engine certificate. Now, he was ready to fly the big planes. According to his personal pilot, flying a jet was not much different from flying the smaller engine planes. The main difference was in the engines and all the moving components.

He had called ahead of time to have his Cessna moved outside the hangar so that he could go out. He took his time doing his pre-flight inspection; even though he was confident his mechanic did that beforehand. Before taking off, he moved his Bentley into the hangar. He prized that car over any of his other possessions and did not want it scratched outside. He had made sure the car looked like he just drove it off the showroom, even though it was almost six months old now.

As he walked out of the hangar, his mechanic walked up to him, "Looks like you have a great day for flying."

"It sure does. I checked the weather last night and again before I headed out. No thunderstorms are predicted for today."

As he bent down to check the landing gear, the mechanic mentioned, "Boss, I did all that when you called and asked me to pull her out of the hangar for you."

"I'm sure you did, just a force of habit, I reckon. See you when I get back."

"Have a safe flight."

He climbed up into the plane and settled into his seat. After putting on his headphones, he checked to make sure the area was clear. Once he confirmed the area was ready for takeoff; he started the engine and taxied to the runway. When he received clearance from the tower, he took one final look around, pushed the throttle forward and began his takeoff roll.

The Cessna took off without a hitch. When he filled out his flight plan last night, he decided that he would fly over the bayous to see how busy they were. He was still trying to figure out where to expand his fishing charter business. A few hours later, he set the plane down on the centerline and taxied back to the hangar.

- - - - - - ●● ● ●● - - - - - - - -

Once back in his car, his thoughts drifted to Lexi. He knew he had to see her. As soon as he walked into the hotel, he scanned the opulent lobby for her. His whole body was tense; his eyes scanned the hotel with the intensity and total focus of a madman. He wondered where she was. She was always fluttering around the lobby.

As he looked around, he noticed that she had done a fantastic job with it. Soon, she may be sent to work on yet another one and his heart sank at the thought of her traveling to yet another city. He preferred her to be here.

Shaking his head, he knew that he should not even be here. She had too much on her mind to consider starting another relationship. Yet, he could not stop the fantasies from playing out in his mind. When he lay in bed at night, he wanted her at his side. If he closed his eyes now, he could picture her laid out on his bed screaming his name as passion consumed her.

He took a deep breath, slowly releasing it as he calmed his racing heart. He forced his body to relax, telling himself that a relationship with Lexi just was not in the cards. But here he was hoping to catch a glimpse of her at work.

Something about the woman brought out a strange, territorial, and protective instinct that kept him coming back to her.

He desperately wanted to tell her just how much he cared for her. Hell, he cared more for her than her ex-husband ever did.

He held back a groan of frustration as he thought about the humor flashing in her eyes when she laughed at something he said, or the way her silky hair escaped from the seductive bun that she wore to work. Even the way her body moved gracefully when she walked appealed to him. She had him caught in her unintentional web; he was a prisoner in her heart. He also had no desire to ruin their friendship either. Instead, it would be better off if he kept their relationship as friends with benefits, but primarily friends.

From the corner of his eye, he felt himself coming to attention as he caught sight of her. Shifting positions, he tried to will his excitement to calm down. His whole body came to life every time he saw her. Just what was it about this woman that made him so edgy and restless? She was the only woman who had this control over him.

He had dated countless women, and slept with most of them, but none of them had ever touched his emotions as she did. Hell, he would prefer to spend time with his computer rather than attending social functions. In truth, the only time he actively sought out a woman was when he needed some physical relief. He always dated women who did not ask for anything in return. That was enough for him; that was until Lexi.

A shudder of rage propelled within him at the thought of Bennett touching her delectable body. A purely feral instinct rose up at the thought of any man touching her. He told himself to get a grip. He could not expect her to remain celibate. It was not her fault that he chose not to make a move.

Could it be the fear of failure that prevented him from making a move on Lexi? He had never failed at anything he attempted. So why didn't he make a move now?

As she gave a quick wave to him, he wondered if maybe it was time for him to take the risk. No, he should get over this crazy obsession he had with her. He had thought making love to her would be enough to quench this never-ending wanting he had for her, but instead it had him wanting more of her.

As he scanned the hotel lobby once more, he noticed that there were plenty of available women here in Springport. Perhaps seeing another woman would take his mind off of Lexi. Except when he looked at other women he immediately compared them to Lexi.

As she walked over his way, he came to realize that he could not handle these animalistic and rampant emotions anymore; he did not like them. He was not used to them; he wanted his sanity back. He wanted to return to his computer and work on his passion for developing computer games without the thought of Lexi taking over his mind. Or better yet, concentrate on his new fishing charter business. Sense. Reason. Control. That was how he functioned. Dammit! He needed to get back to a normal state of mind.

With a glint in her eye, she kissed him affectionately on the cheek. "What a surprise to see you here." She placed a perfectly manicured hand on his forearm; her burgundy nails glistened against his forearm.

"I stopped by to see how you are doing. I was hoping we could go out for supper if you feel up to it."

When she smiled up at him, his heart skipped a beat. The smile on her lips promised more than just dinner; it promised a night to remember. His body surged to life. Looking at his Rolex, he asked, "How about I pick you up here at five thirty?"

"That should give me enough time to finish up."

As he watched her leave, he tried his best not to carry the vision of her lush breasts and perfect derriere walking seductively away from him.

At five thirty, she walked out of her office and greeted him with another one of her fantastic smiles. "I don't know about you, but I am starving."

Extending his arm, he informed her, "Well then, let's get you something to eat."

Once at the restaurant, they each ordered the filet mignon and butter poached lobster, and they discussed their day. As Lexi cut into the steak, she said, "This is delicious. Thank you for this special treat." After dinner, she indulged in a piece of chocolate mousse pie while he sipped his Maker's Mark whiskey. He watched as the amber liquor swirled in his glass before setting it down on the table decisively. Looking into her eyes, he asked, "Would you care to dance?"

Pushing her plate away, she smiled over at him, "I thought you would never ask."

The band was playing a romantic song, perfect for seduction. As he led her to the dance floor, he noticed that it was practically empty. Taking her into his arms, he pulled her body close to his. The highlights in her auburn hair glittered under the muted lights. He told himself it was the one dance; it could only be one dance.

They moved together naturally as they swayed skillfully to the music. He watched as her lips parted as she sighed seductively before placing her head on his shoulder.

He found himself losing himself in her. What possessed him into asking her to dance? Why was he torturing himself? He adjusted her body against him, trying to mold the softness of her against him.

Chapter 28

Lexi used her feet to propel herself in the swing, extending her tan legs to go a little higher. The sun streamed through the trees onto her face. This past month, visiting the park had become a favorite pastime.

As she swung, she daydreamed about what her baby would be like. As he or she gave her a swift kick, she placed a hand on her ever growing stomach. Lexi rubbed her belly, "You are a lucky baby. Your mother loves you very much."

Lexi felt a fluttering in her stomach and she continued to croon words of love.

It would not be too many more months before this child made its entrance into the world, and she could not wait.

A little girl's voice interrupted her thoughts, "Excuse me, but are you going to have a baby?"

Lexi looked down at the girl with a mass of wild, unruly curls. "Yes, I am."

"Do you mind if I touch your tummy? Mommy says that I have to ask first."

She took the little girl's hand and placed it on her stomach. At that moment, the baby gave a nice solid kick. The girl giggled at the feeling. "My mommy will have a baby soon, too. She says that I am getting a little brother." Taking a breath before continuing, she asked, "Do you know what you are having?"

Shaking her head, Lexi told her, "No, I sure don't."

The little girl sighed, "Oh, that is too bad." The child leaned in closer, "You see, I don't want a brother. Boys are gross. I want a little sister to play with. I was kind of hoping you wanted to trade with my mommy."

Lexi smiled at the little girl's honesty, "I am sorry, honey. I bet you will fall in love with your little brother once you see him. Boys can be fun, too, you know."

"I guess, but I really hope he doesn't like to play with bugs like Johnny does."

Lexi chuckled as she asked, "Oh. Who is Johnny?"

"He is in my class, but he is so gross. He is always catching bugs and chasing us with them. I sure hope my brother doesn't act like him."

"Well, perhaps you can teach your brother how not to act."

The little girl placed an index finger on her tiny chin as she contemplated what Lexi just told her, "Hmm. Maybe so. I sure hope so."

As Lexi walked back to the hotel, she laughed at the conversation she just had with the precocious little girl. Being the youngest, and her only other sibling an older brother, she had not been around too many children.

If she wanted to be honest with herself, she never considered having children. It had come as a shock when she learned that she was pregnant. On the way back to work, she stopped by the café and bought a few chocolate filled beignets. She had craved sweets, and these satisfied that craving. As soon as the cashier handed her the order, she sank her teeth into the warm pastry and let out an appreciative moan. The chocolate and fried doughnut hit all the right taste buds. She took a sip of her decaffeinated café au lait to wash down the sweet pastry and continued her walk back to the hotel.

Once she reached the hotel, her phone rang. It was one of her friends from college who only called when she needed something.

"Hey Lexi, this is Jennifer. I'm not catching you at a bad time am I?"

"No, you are fine, Jennifer. Can I help you with something?"

"Well, to be honest with you, I do need something. You see, Blake asked me to marry him and as soon as I thought of the wedding; I thought of the beautiful ballroom at the hotel where you work. It would be just perfect to hold the reception, but I wasn't sure if the date I wanted is open."

As she listened to Jennifer go on about all the wedding plans, she found it hard to be happy for her. She listened halfheartedly as Jennifer told her about Blake's proposal. She had to admit that it sounded romantic. He managed to do all the right things from the candlelit supper, complete with wine and a special dessert. Once in her office, she confirmed that the date Jennifer requested was open. Jennifer eagerly asked, "Would you be a dear and write us down for that date? I will be by tomorrow to take care of the deposit and anything else you need."

After saying goodbye to Jennifer, Lexi left the office to go home. All she wanted was to curl up in bed and fall sound asleep.

She lovingly rubbed her belly as the baby kicked. Her heart swelled with love, "I don't ever want you to think I regret your birth. It may be just you and me Babykins, but we will be just fine."

She often wondered if Bennett ever had genuine feelings for her. She thought he hung the moon, but that illusion had been long since shattered. Once again, she shook off the feeling of inadequacy that had plagued her ever since Bennett informed her he wanted a divorce. Her heart broke when she learned his mistress was pregnant, and he wanted nothing to do with their child. He insisted he had no place in his life for her or their baby. April and their baby were his new life. Well, she hoped what they said was true and once a cheater always a cheater.

She would not venture into a new romance. Never again would she risk her heart to another man. Bennett's cruel betrayal and the words he threw at her cured her of any romantic notions. Some people were destined to live happily ever after, but that was not in her future.

She learned that lesson the hard way. She had nothing to offer a man. Rubbing her stomach, "You will love me forever though, won't you?"

She never thought she could love another human being as much as she loved this child growing inside of her. When she looked in the mirror, she could see the overwhelming glow of love radiating from her. She would cherish this child and never stop loving it, no matter who its father was. She may hate Bennett for what he did to her, but she could never hate him for giving her this child.

Chapter 29

Lexi crossed off another item on her list to do this afternoon. She had two tasks remaining before she could call it a day.

She turned back to her keyboard and typed the rest of the report due today. Just as she was ready to leave, her boss sent her another email. Letting out a soft groan, she quickly read it and saw he was coming to town on Monday to check on things. She had yet to tell him about her pregnancy, so it looked as if she had no choice but to make the announcement on Monday. Hopefully, he was impressed enough with her work and would not replace her while she was on maternity leave.

As she prepared to leave for the day, her cell phone rang. "Lexi, I hope I didn't catch you at a bad time?"

At the sound of her divorce attorney's voice, she grimaced, "Only if you aren't calling to give me more bad news."

"No, actually it is good news. Everything is finalized. The divorce papers are signed and filed. You are officially a single woman again."

This was the moment she had been waiting for and suddenly she found herself speechless. Now that it was here, she did not know what to say.

"Lexi, are you there? Is everything okay?"

Snapping herself out of her mood, she said hurriedly, "Yes, I'm sorry. I don't know why, but the news caught me off guard."

"That's okay. I have been in this business long enough to know that these proceedings pack an emotional punch."

"You can say that again."

"If Bennett continues harassing you, give me a call. I can get you a restraining order in no time."

She heard the underlying vehemence in the divorce attorney's voice. Something told her that on more than one occasion it was necessary. Besides, Bennett had been extremely childish about the divorce and Lexi's pregnancy.

- - - - - • • • • • ● • • • • • - - - -

"Seriously, Lexi, why are you making me sit through this chick movie?" Kyle complained as the couple on the screen struggled with their attraction to each other.

Laughingly, she answered, "Because it was my turn to pick the movie. Besides, it is only fair. You made me sit through that horrible horror movie last time. Consider us even."

"Fine," he grumbled, "but I need another beer. Do you want anything?"

Shaking her head no, she lifted her legs from his lap so he could stand up.

As she continued to watch the movie, she wished that her life had some resemblance to this movie. Instead, here she was divorced, pregnant, and alone. If it weren't for Kyle, she did not know what she would do. He had been her rock.

Like today, he knew she would be depressed with her divorce being finalized, and he insisted they go out. Since she did not want to be around other people, they went to the movie store, picked out a movie, and came back to her house. This had been just the mindless distraction she needed. Although, perhaps a horror movie would have been better. The movie reminded her how much romance was lacking in her life.

The one thing this divorce had taught her was that life always took unexpected turns. Never again would she be blinded by love. She gave everything to her ex-husband and look where that got her. It would take her broken heart a long time to heal. During that time, she would focus all her love on this child she was getting ready to bring into the world.

Kyle pulled her into his warm embrace. "Ah, honey, I wish there was something that I could do, but at least that part of your life is officially over."

"It's not the divorce that bothers me, but the way Bennett handled this whole matter. If April weren't pregnant and insisted on Bennett marrying her right away, I wonder if this whole thing would be resolved this fast. We fought for months over stipulations for the divorce and then, suddenly, April gets Bennett to sign everything. Was I just too weak around him? The whole time we were married he never once listened to what I had to say, everything had to be his way. This woman came in and made him bend to her will."

Shrugging his shoulders, he said, "I don't know, maybe they are truly in love or Bennett is blinded by his love for her."

"Maybe April has something good on Bennett and she can put pressure on him to do whatever she likes." Laughing at the thought of Bennett's life being miserable, "Well, at least he is her problem now. The divorce papers are signed, and they have their marriage license."

"So, it doesn't bother you that he is marrying April?"

Shivering just at the thought of how her life might have turned out if she had stayed with the two-timing bastard, "Nope, not one bit." Rubbing her stomach, she reminded him, "This is the one good thing that came out of my marriage with Bennett."

"Okay, enough of this depressing talk. Have you picked out baby names?"

"Nothing definite yet. I have been trying out different names, but nothing seems to fit."

"Promise me that you won't give this child a name that will be difficult to grow up with."

Shaking her head as she laughed, "Okay, I promise I won't."

Looking at Lexi, he leaned down to kiss her. Lexi continued the kiss with the same amount of fervor he showed. Delightful sensations ran through her body as the kiss continued.

He pulled her onto his lap, molding her body against the hard play of his muscles. As the pulsating pleasure swept through her body, she could hardly catch her breath. Her arms wrapped around his neck as the hunger for him enveloped her. The warmth of his body heated her blood to boiling.

As he broke the kiss, he swiped a thumb over her swollen, damp lips. "I keep telling myself that I am not going to take advantage of you tonight, but when I am with you, I seem to have no willpower."

Instead of answering, Lexi brushed her lips against his. The strong arms holding her showed just a hint of tender emotion for this woman he was coming to love.

Lexi lost herself in his kiss. Wrapping her arms around him, little zings of pleasure surged through her as she brimmed with passionate energy.

Was there a chance for a happily ever after with Kyle? Could she let love wrap her in its warm embrace once more? She was not sure she could take that chance though. If Kyle walked away from her, she would lose him forever. That would be far worse than when Bennett ended their relationship.

She was already feeling more for Kyle than was safe. For her to become entangled with her best friend may not be in her best interest.

No, the last thing Lexi needed was to ruin her friendship with Kyle. Instead, she needed to concentrate on this baby she was carrying. There were plenty of single mothers who managed just fine without anyone's help. She planned to be one of them.

She held back a tear. She could not afford to lose Kyle. No, instead she would be independent, and would remain independent.

Chapter 30

Lexi groaned as the alarm clock went off. She threw off the covers then swung her feet to the floor. She was in such a hurry that she knocked over the water bottle sitting too close to the edge of her nightstand and cursed as she grabbed a towel from the bathroom.

Her boss would be at the hotel in an hour. She did not have much time to dress and get to work. Perhaps she should have listened to her gut and slept there last night. As soon as she stepped out of the shower, she wrapped a towel around her hair before padding to the kitchen. She poured herself a cup of coffee and toasted a bagel before going back to the bathroom to blow dry her hair.

She rushed through applying her makeup and threw on a navy blue business suit that hid her pregnancy as best as she could.

Just as she finished getting dressed, her doorbell rang. She opened her door and was surprised to see Kyle there. He was dressed in a dark business suit and checking his smartphone. It irked her how he could stand there looking so business-like and unruffled. "I thought you may like a ride into work this morning."

Reaching up to kiss him, she said, "You are my hero. You do know that, don't you?"

"Well, I do aim to please."

"You are the absolute best. I am running late and my boss is coming to the hotel this morning." As she rushed around the house, she was trying to finish getting dressed.

He smiled over at her, "Here, let me help you." He reached down and fixed one of the buttons that she missed as she managed to latch her necklace. As they walked out the door, she was still attempting to style her hair because several unruly curls refused to cooperate.

- - - - - ●●● ● ●●●● - - - -

As Lexi left work, her phone rang. When Lexi saw that it was her divorce attorney calling, she almost panicked. "Good afternoon, I hope you're not calling to say there are some problems with the divorce papers."

"No, I was just calling to check and see how you were doing. I know Bennett had been giving you a hard time and I wanted to make sure that everything was okay."

"I'm fine. Hopefully, now that the divorce is finalized Bennett will get on with his life."

"Well, since things ended on a sour note, if he harasses you, let me know and I will get a restraining order."

"I appreciate that, but I don't think it's going to be necessary. I am hoping Bennett will start focusing on his new life with his new girlfriend."

"Well, if you ever need anything, you know how to get in touch with me."

As Lexi said her goodbyes and hung up, the one thing she hoped for is that she would never need another divorce attorney.

One positive upside of the divorce was that Lexi no longer had to deal with her overbearing mother in law.

- - - - - - - - - - ● - - - - - - - - - - -

That night as Kyle brought her home, they went out for supper first. It had been a long day, and Lexi wanted to unwind. The only good thing that had happened was that her boss had taken the news of her pregnancy well. Now, if she could only shake the unsettling feeling that Bennett would be waiting at home for her. She was in no mood to listen to his rantings about an abortion. He had been persistent on the matter since finding out she was pregnant.

As they walked into the restaurant, she looked around. "You have been keeping all the good restaurants to yourself. I love the atmosphere here."

As he escorted her inside, he told her, "Wait until you taste the food. I hope the wait isn't long."

Both were pleasantly surprised to learn there was only a ten-minute wait. While the maître d walked them past several couples seated at cozy candlelit tables in the well-appointed restaurant, she came to realize that this was what she needed tonight.

They were seated at an intimate table at the window that overlooked the river. A few people were dancing to a slow jazz song, while others simply enjoyed the romantic setting in front of them.

Staring out over the water, she slipped into a trance as she watched the full, breathtaking moon reflected on the water. It created graceful ripples of shimmering waves against the dark water.

As she perused the menu, she asked, "Everything looks delicious. What do you recommend?"

"The shrimp and crab boulettes are excellent for an appetizer, but the Oysters En Brochette is exceptional, as well. The chef wraps select oysters in bacon and fries them to perfection."

As they decided on what they wanted for the appetizers, their waitress appeared, "I am sorry to keep you waiting. We are extremely busy tonight."

Kyle smiled up at the young girl, "It does look as if you have a full house this evening."

She nodded her head in agreement. "Have you decided what you would like or do you need a few more minutes?"

Kyle replied, "I would like a Maker's Mark Manhattan, and she would like an Arnold Palmer. For our appetizers, we would like the Oysters En Brochette."

"Of course, sir. I would also like to tell you about our entrée special. The chef has fixed a fried eggplant layered with shrimp stuffing and then topped with a creamy pesto sauce brimming with shrimp and crabmeat. It is served with fresh roasted asparagus."

Lexi could feel her mouth watering already, "I am not sure about you Kyle, but I will have the special. That sounds too tempting to pass up."

As Kyle handed the waitress their menus, he agreed, "I will have the filet mignon steak topped with lump crabmeat and mushrooms sautéed in butter. For the side dish, may I please have the loaded stuffed baked potato?"

"Very good, sir. That is an excellent choice."

As they waited for their cocktails and appetizers, they became absorbed in pleasant conversation.

It was not long before the waitress set their drinks and appetizers in front of them. As always, the food teased her taste buds and had her craving more. As they enjoyed the delicious food and soothing jazz music, she felt herself relaxing from the stress of the day.

The waitress cleared away their dinner dishes and asked, "Would you care for dessert?"

Lexi had been eyeing the dessert cart since walking in the door. "I am not sure which one I want to try. They all look simply divine."

The waitress exclaimed, "I would recommend our sweet potato beignets. They are filled with a decadent chocolate and topped with an orange hazelnut glaze. It is the chef's newest creation. Everyone just raves about them."

"Oh, I have to try those then. This baby has me craving beignets." Lexi looked over at Kyle, "I may be sweet-talked into sharing."

"I already have my dessert picked out, but it has to wait until later on."

After finishing the dessert, he held his hand out and asked, "Would you care to dance?"

She leaned her head on his chest as they danced to the soft jazz music that was playing. As she moved against his body to the music, all the troubles plaguing her seemed to dissolve from her mind. The moonlight glistening off of the dark rolling water helped set the mood for romance.

With his arms around her, she looked up at him. Their lips met slowly at first.

He completely intoxicated her as no man had done, which both excited and frightened her. She fell in love with Bennett quickly and look where that got her.

After paying the bill, he slipped his arm around her and guided her to the car. She sighed in contentment and stated, "This has been a wonderful evening." As they walked back to the car, the moon hung low over the river creating a breathtaking view. They strolled contentedly arm in arm, enjoying the starry night.

As he opened the door for her, he kissed her once more; she found her arms moving up to his neck – not wanting the kiss to end. She whispered against his lips, "I don't want to spend tonight alone."

He looked down at her with lust clearly in his eyes. The drive home took an eternity. As soon as they were in the door, he pulled Lexi close to him. He took her mouth in a gentle caress, his breath skirted her lips. Only when her mouth became pliant and willing did he deepen the kiss, thrusting his tongue inside to dance with hers. They kissed with such passion that it ignited a spark deep inside of her. She loved how he made her feel wanted, needed and desired.

Chapter 31

Lexi tucked a stray tendril of hair behind her ear before letting out a frustrated breath. She could do this, she had to do this.

Cooking could not be that hard. Her mother had prepared Thanksgiving dinner for years now, and Lexi refused to give her mother another chance to point out her failures.

She looked around the room and groaned when she noticed that the kitchen was in complete disarray. There was flour everywhere as she tried desperately to prepare the pie crusts for the apple dumplings. She still had to get everything ready for the cranberry sauce and prepare the sweet potato soufflé.

If nothing else, they had a turkey to eat and at least it smelled delicious. She had read recipe after recipe until she found what she thought was the best one. She created a special marinade to inject in the turkey that was comprised of melted butter, her favorite seasoning, garlic, and a dash of hot sauce and marinated it overnight. When she slipped the turkey into the oven, she felt confident about the way she had prepped the bird.

The yeast rolls were rising, and she was determined to finish the apple dumplings. The sweet potatoes should be done in a few minutes and from there she would prepare the soufflé. The rice was cooking for the dirty rice, and she also had cornbread baking so that she could make a small cornbread stuffing.

All she asked her mother to bring was the oyster dressing. As brave as Lexi felt tackling Thanksgiving dinner, she had no intention of fixing her dad's favorite dish. Just the smell of raw oysters sent her stomach rolling.

She hoped the meal turned out well. Both her mother and brother had laughed when she announced that she wanted to prepare Thanksgiving dinner. Her mother started calling early this week to make sure Lexi had bought everything that she needed, reminding her often that by Wednesday the stores would be packed with people and running low on certain items. She had to tell her brother's wife, Janie, that she did not need her help either. No matter how much they insisted, she was determined to do this alone.

Apparently, they thought that with the divorce, her pregnancy, and work she was incapable of handling anything. She wanted to prove them wrong. More importantly, she wanted to prove to herself that she could do this.

While married to Bennett, she rarely cooked extravagant meals. Usually, their meals consisted of take out and simple things, although, they tended to eat out most weekends.

As her mind drifted to memories of Bennett, she shook herself to erase those thoughts. She refused to fall into the remorse trap again. It was not good for the baby to have a depressed mother. She should focus on the positive things in her life. She needed to concentrate on being happy and not dwelling on the past. As the baby gave her a quick kick, she smiled. Even if she did raise this baby alone, she had enough love for the two of them.

Looking over everything, she realized the one thing she forgot to purchase was wine. Being pregnant, alcohol was the furthest thing from her mind. She sent Kyle a text, "Would you please bring a bottle of wine?"

It wasn't long before she received a text back, "Are you planning on getting me drunk and having your way with me?"

She laughed at his comment. She would love to have her way with him, but that was not going to happen today with her parents and family at the house. She prayed that this went well, and that her mom behaved.

They were all comfortable with Kyle and he had promised to spend a few hours here before heading to his parents' house for their dinner. Her parents liked to eat early, where his parents preferred to eat late.

He would be her security blanket while her family was here.

- - - - - - - - - - ● - - - - - - - - - -

After she had cleaned the kitchen, she made sure her dining room and the living room was ready. They would be spread out, but comfortable.

As she was pulling the turkey out of the oven, her phone rang, "Happy Thanksgiving, Mom."

"We are coming over a little early in case you need help with any last minute details." She heard the worry and doubt in her mother's voice.

She counted to ten, willing herself the patience to make it through the day and hoped that her voice did not sound as frazzled as she felt. "Mom, you are welcome to come over, but I have everything taken care of. The turkey is resting, and everything else will be done shortly."

"Are you sure honey? The oyster dressing is ready, and I made a pecan pie."

"Thank you, Mom, but the pie isn't necessary. I made Grandma's apple dumplings. I know how much dad enjoys them."

"Oh, well then, okay. What about vanilla ice cream? Do we need to pick that up?"

"I have that also. I made sure to get Dad's favorite brand."

"Well then, it sounds like you have taken care of everything. We will see you in a little while. By the way, did you change your mind about going Black Friday shopping with Janie and me?"

She cringed at the thought of shopping with those two. While her mom and Janie did not see eye to eye on most things, shopping was one passion they had in common — especially bargain shopping. However, even more disturbing was waking up at an ungodly hour to see what deals were available.

"No, y'all do not need to drag a pregnant woman along."

"Well then, see you soon."

As she hung up the phone, tears built up. "I told you we should run away for the holidays."

She turned around and saw Kyle leaning against the kitchen door. His eyes twinkled with mischief as he placed the bottle of wine in the fridge. While he looked around the kitchen, he told her, "I am impressed with you. I had half expected to walk into a mess."

Laughing, she admitted, "If you had been here earlier, you would have seen a pure mess. The dishwasher has run non-stop, and I even used the laundry room sink to help me keep up with the dishes that needed to be hand washed. I used the tops of the washer and dryer to dry the pots and pans on, but at least I kept up with the dishes. It took forever to clean the floor, but it is done." As she took down the wine glasses, she told Kyle, "Right now, I wish I could have a glass or two of wine. My mom has called nonstop wondering if she could do anything. I don't think she has confidence in me to pull this off."

Before she felt the heat of his body or the sound of his breath, she sensed him behind her. The back of her neck prickled with anticipation. As he massaged her shoulders, he said, "You need to relax. It doesn't need to be perfect."

"Yes, it does. I am tired of my family thinking I am a failure at everything I do. My mom loves reminding me of my most recent failure, my marriage."

Wrapping his arms around her, he brought her closer to him. She felt the power of his muscles as the heat of his embrace moved through her body. His hands caressed her growing stomach. He buried his head in her hair as he inhaled her scent.

The moment his arms wrapped her in his embrace, he forgot that he should resist her. "Bennett leaving you for another woman had nothing to do with you. That was Bennett's fault. He is a scumbag. You did nothing wrong. You need to remember that."

"I know that, but a part of me keeps thinking I should have tried to be a better wife. Maybe if I had paid more attention to him or learned how to do more womanly things, he wouldn't have found someone else."

"Trust me, you are all woman. Bennett was an idiot."

Suddenly, she realized that he was holding her close. She felt his hot breath on her neck. A shudder of pleasure ran through her as she struggled to pull her thoughts together.

Slipping her hands around his neck, she wove her fingers through his hair as she tilted her head up. As Kyle bent down to kiss her, the doorbell rang. She muttered, "I bet it is my mom. She always knows when I am about to do something."

Her mother entered the house as soon as Lexi opened the door. "I thought you could use an extra pair of hands."

Lexi's father was shaking his head, "Shannon, I have a feeling that Lexi has it under control." Giving her a kiss on her cheek her dad said, "It smells wonderful in here, honey. Where do you want the dressing?"

Leading him into the kitchen as they trailed behind her mother, "You can put it on the kitchen counter."

When they entered the kitchen, Kyle was helping himself to the crudités plate, "There is nothing to worry about Mrs. Bertrand. Lexi has everything under control."

Lexi's mom gave a startled gasp when she noticed Kyle, "Oh, Kyle, I didn't know you were coming."

"I couldn't miss Lexi cooking her first Thanksgiving dinner, now could I?"

Before anyone replied, the doorbell rang. Lexi was surprised to see that her brother and his family were early also. Groaning, she asked, "What's wrong? You didn't think I could pull it off either?"

Janie gave Lexi a kiss on the cheek, "Heavens no. Your brother was driving me nuts. He is worried that he will miss some stupid football game." Walking toward the kitchen, she went on, "I know that you said you would prepare the whole meal, but since we came over early, I made a pizza cheese dip, spinach dip, and cookies. The kids are totally addicted to this pizza dip, but they eat more crackers than dip."

As she made room on the counter for the food Janie brought, she replied, "You didn't need to go through all that trouble, but I do appreciate it."

Janie waved her hands in the air, "Please, the dips were easy to whip up; besides, my two kids have turned into gluttons. I can't seem to fill them up. It looks like they are getting ready to go through another growth spurt." Janie lovingly rubbed Lexi's belly, "Soon you will find out just what all this is like. I can't wait to meet this little one." As Janie helped herself to the spinach dip she brought, she said, "You should know that I am really impressed with you wanting to tackle cooking Thanksgiving dinner. When I was carrying Grant, I couldn't stand the sight of food, and with Madison, I was constantly tired."

Before she replied, her brother's booming voice called out, "Kyle, my man. You got dragged into this, too."

Kyle laughed, "I wouldn't miss this for anything."

Jason gave Lexi a kiss on her cheek before fixing himself a plate of crackers and dip, "It all looks great sis. I can't wait to dig in."

Lexi laughed, "Oh yeah, so why are you fixing yourself a plate to snack on?"

"Game's on; besides, I can eat this and still make room for everything you cooked. It smells damn good in here." Turning to Kyle, "Come on bro, let's get out of this hen house and watch the game."

Kyle winked over at Lexi before heading out of the kitchen. Janie caught the look Kyle gave Lexi and immediately asked, "Oh boy. He is hot. Is there something going on between you and Mr. Handsome?"

That comment ruffled her mother's feathers. She retorted, "Lexi doesn't have time to start another relationship. She needs to concentrate on getting back together with her baby's father."

"Mom, please stop. I know you mean well, but what Bennett and I once had is over." Fighting back the tears, "He no longer loves or wants me. He does not want this baby!"

Janie waved a hand through the air, "Oh please, like hell she does! If you ask me, Bennett got off easy. If it had been me, I would have cut off that one-eyed worm of his and crammed it down his throat. And that's just the beginning."

Lexi snorted out a chuckle as her mother put a hand over her heart, "Janie, that isn't the right attitude with regards to this situation."

Janie ignored her mother-in-law, "Truthfully Lexi, don't you feel a little sorry for his new woman? I think you are the lucky one. I have seen him prancing around in those Lycra shorts he likes to wear. Really, men shouldn't wear things like that if they don't have a package to show us."

Lexi laughed at her sister-in-law, "He may not have been overly endowed, but he knew how to use what

God gave him. I couldn't complain about that part of our life."

Janie shrugged her shoulders, "You could have fooled me." She tilted back in her chair to make sure the men were still watching the football game, "Now, something tells me Mr. Handsome in there is well endowed and would leave a woman very satisfied."

Lexi felt her cheeks turning red, "I wouldn't know."

"Well, the two of y'all have been friends for a long time. You should look into being friends with benefits. Your hormones will begin to surge soon, and you will want to satisfy that itch. Trust me, there are no mechanical instruments that will satisfy you like a man." Checking once more to make sure the men were not coming, Janie leaned in and whispered to Lexi, "Besides, I saw the way he was looking at you earlier. If you want to jump his bones, he won't turn you down."

With a carefree laugh, Lexi stated, "Trust me, he just sees me as a friend."

Lexi's mother gasped, "Young lady, this is not an appropriate conversation to be having."

Shrugging her shoulders, "I don't see why not. We have all had sex, and I think Lexi needs to let her hair down and have some fun."

Lexi laughed. She had never seen Janie this way. Lexi whispered in her ear, "What has gotten into you?"

"I think that you got the raw end of the deal. I chewed your brother's ass out and told him exactly what would happen to him if I ever caught him cheating on me. He had a new reckoning with that conversation. I also informed him that Bennett has always been an ass, and I didn't know what you saw in him. I had kept my mouth shut since you seemed to love him."

Lexi nodded her head, "I honestly thought we were in love and happy. It has been hard coming to terms with the fact that Bennett never loved me."

"Honey, the only person Bennett will ever love is himself. Consider yourself lucky he is out of your life. You should be thankful that he does not want to be part of your child's life also. Can you imagine what this child would be like with a role model like Bennett as a father?"

A shudder of disappointment ran through Lexi at the thought of her child turning out like Bennett. "Oh, my goodness, I never once considered that. Perhaps I am lucky."

Before the conversation could continue, Lexi's mom interrupted, "Well, it is time to get started with our Thanksgiving meal so Kyle can join his parents." Turning toward Lexi, she stated, "Can we all fit in the dining room?"

Lexi nodded her head, "I have everything set up. I fixed the children a table in the living room so that they can watch television if they want."

Jason must have overheard the conversation, "Well, I say that since the game is still on, the men eat in the living room if they want."

Lexi's mom lectured her brother, "Now Jason, you know that we have always eaten in the dining room as a family."

He groaned, "But this is a really good game. I hate to miss it; besides, I am sure that Lexi won't mind if we eat in here, do you?"

Lexi shrugged her shoulders, "I say let him eat where he wants."

Janie nodded her head in agreement, "Besides, that way he can watch the kids as they eat, and I can actually eat a meal in peace. Now, that would make it a great Thanksgiving."

Lexi could not help but smile as her mother threw her hands up in the air. Shannon Bertrand despised when things did not go her way, and this Thanksgiving was completely out of her control.

As Lexi was sitting down with her plate, Kyle sat in the chair next to her. "Take a breath and relax. Look around you. Everyone is having a great time."

For the first time that day, Lexi took a moment to observe her surroundings. The other men and the children were talking and laughing in the living room; her mother was mumbling to herself and Janie kept looking over at Lexi with a huge "I told you so" smile on her face. Perhaps, this day would go better than she predicted.

Chapter 32

Kyle looked around the crowded room and forced himself not to yawn. He dreaded attending events where everyone drank too much, laughed too loud, and tried far too hard to impress each other.

As he looked around, he was genuinely impressed with the fabulous job Lexi and her crew did in getting everything ready for tonight's gala. The ambiance was elegant and entirely fitting those attending. Everywhere he looked, he saw people dressed to impress. As if the most important thing tonight was to outshine everyone else. It was as if each woman's clothing and jewelry surpassed the rest.

He took a long, hard swallow of his whiskey as he caught glimpses of several women eyeing him hard. He wished Lexi would hurry up and get here. The crowd seemed to be increasing in size and noise. Even with everything going on, he was bored out of his mind.

He groaned as Gabrielle Arnold came up to him and clung to his arm as if her life depended on it. "Kyle, I am glad that you could make it to the benefit, but why are you standing all by yourself?"

She moved in closer to him, making sure to push up her assets provocatively. This was one of the biggest reasons he despised these things. The women tended to latch onto him as if he was the last man on earth. Gabrielle was severely annoying him with the way she bit her lower lip as she pouted. She was merely waiting for him to make a move. Hell would freeze over before he allowed this woman to warm his bed.

He thought by this age, he would be married, but instead, he was still one of the most sought-after bachelors. Most of his time was spent running from women, not toward women.

He realized how funny life was. Lexi had always been his best friend, his solace. Bennett had complained about the time she took from him, and it was that very complaint that led Kyle to introduce the two of them. He had hoped that they would all get along. However, he did not expect the two to get along as well as they did. Would their lives have turned out differently if he never introduced Bennett to Lexi?

- - - - - - - - ● - - - - - - - - - -

Lexi was running late as usual. She had a meeting scheduled for seven o'clock and woke up at six thirty. Jumping out of bed in a panic, she rushed to get ready. She halfway dried her hair and hoped that by the time she arrived at work it would be dry.

As she looked through her closet, she had a hard time finding anything that would fit her. Once again, she needed to purchase a few more clothes. Giving up on a suit, she found a dress and slipped a lightweight sweater over it.

As she raced to her car, she became flushed. To make matters worse, her stomach was already growling, and she had no time to grab anything to eat. She made a mental note to call and have the restaurant deliver something to her office this morning.

On top of that, Kyle had sent her several text messages requesting that she please attend a benefit he had to go to tonight. He had been there for her lately, and she felt this was something she must do. Now, she crossed her fingers that at least one dress in her closet fit her because there was no way she would have time to run to a boutique today.

She had been so absorbed in her work today that she never once realized the time. Now, she was indeed running late for the second time today and had to rush if she wanted to get dressed in time for the benefit.

She had been extremely grateful when Kyle sent her a message earlier stating that he was taking care of her attire for tonight. When the package arrived, she was more than pleased. He had indeed taken care of everything for her.

As she rushed up to her hotel room, she called room service to have a turkey sandwich brought up ASAP. She had skipped lunch and was starving. By the time she jumped in and out of the shower, being mindful not to get her hair wet, her sandwich had arrived. She finished eating her sandwich while applying her makeup.

By the time she buckled the ankle straps on the silver heeled sandals Kyle had picked to go with the green cocktail dress, she was running fifteen minutes late. While in the elevator, she caught her reflection in the mirror and realized she forgot to put her hair up. If she went back upstairs, she would be ridiculously late. She would have to wear it down and pray by the end of the night it did not resemble one big rat's nest.

When she saw Kyle, she knew that he was miserable. Kissing him affectionately on the cheek, she told him, "Sorry I'm late."

"Thankfully, you arrived before any of these women started to draw blood from the claws they dug into me."

She wrapped her hands around his arm, "You poor baby. Well, I am here now, so let's see if they will leave you alone."

He leaned down and kissed her, making sure not to mess up her makeup. He whispered in her ear, "You look absolutely gorgeous. I am the luckiest man here tonight."

"Flattery just might get you everywhere."

"Oh yeah? Hmm, sounds very promising."

"Easy, big boy. The night is still young. Although, you do get extra points for the outfit. I feel like a princess."

"I didn't want to give you any excuse to leave me with these barracudas."

"Well, you can pick my clothes out any time. You have excellent taste."

She sighed as she looked around at the crowd. She could not do this on a routine basis. All around her, trophy wives hung on the arms of their older husbands, and the women wore exceedingly low cut dresses to show off the boobs their husbands in all probability bought them. The expensive clothes required pairing with the fancy jewels which they all seemed to wear. Most of the women had diamonds and other valuable stones dripping off of them, which were undoubtedly worth a small fortune, possibly valued for more than their houses. She saw diamonds the size of golf balls on several ladies' hands.

The band was currently playing soft jazz music, and the dance floor was packed. So far, it looked as if everyone was thoroughly enjoying themselves. The food and booze flowed freely. The bite-size beef Wellingtons were out of this world as were the crab cakes.

They ended up staying at the benefit for over three hours. Toward the end of the night, fatigue won out, and all she wanted to do was crawl into bed and fall fast asleep.

They were getting ready to leave when she caught a glimpse of Bennett and April. They arrived later than her, but everyone here was probably comparing Lexi to April. When Lexi looked over at April, she could not deny that even being pregnant she was a stunning woman. She carried her pregnancy weight well. With Lexi, the weight seemed to be focusing on her stomach and her breasts. Her breasts had already increased another cup size, and she was not even in her last trimester.

When she caught a glimpse of April's ring finger, she had to bite down on her tongue. Did Bennett purchase that ring while Lexi was still paying their bills? It would infuriate her to find out that she bought that ring for April.

Hurt and rage rose in her chest like a tidal wave and completely overwhelmed her. Scenes from the past several months rushed through her mind. The betrayal, the heartbreak, meetings with her divorce attorney, the upheaval, the sleepless nights, and all the STD tests.

At one time, she loved Bennett with all her heart; she never once thought about any of his faults. Now, whenever given the chance, he brought up any faults he found in her. He did nothing but ridicule her lately.

She knew he was coming here tonight, but it rubbed her the wrong way seeing him with her. It was one thing to bear the humiliation of her husband kicking her to the curb for this… this woman, and she used that term loosely, but having to endure watching him parade her all over the room became almost too much. Was he deliberately trying to rub it in her face?

Just watching them had her mind running off into wild tangents. She conjured up visions of the two of them tangled up in the sheets while performing various erotic positions.

Kyle put his arms around her and whispered into her ear, "He isn't worth it."

"I know. It's not that I still love him; it's just that he seems so dang happy with her."

"His betrayal is going to make it hard for you to trust another man isn't it?"

Grimacing at just the thought of offering her heart to another man, "You are the only man I trust."

"Ah, but you don't trust me with your heart. If I asked you to marry me right now, to give me your heart, would you?"

Her eyes rested on his face with caution, "I'm not sure. I try not to be bitter because of him, but it is hard."

He embraced her a little harder, "It hasn't turned you bitter, but I do find that you are a little wary."

She laughed at him, "You are just as bad as me you know. You fear the women coming on to you so you ask your pregnant friend to show up so that women will leave you alone. It isn't as if you are actively searching for a soul mate either. When was the last time you gave someone your heart?"

"Ah, but unlike you, I have not had a tragic relationship. I am leery of all women because when they see me, they see my money; besides, I am not good at relationships."

"Well, I guess that is something else that we have in common. It appears that I am not very good at relationships either."

He kissed her on the top of her head, "Yes you are. It is just that you had someone abuse that love you gave him. You married the wrong man is all."

- - - - - - - - ● - - - - - - - - -

An hour later, they were lying on her hotel bed, watching a movie and waiting for the Chinese food to be delivered. She had changed out of her dress and into a comfortable robe.

Once their food had arrived, he took off his suit jacket and tie before settling down next to her on the bed. After finishing with their food, he pulled her close to him. As he wrapped his arm around her waist to watch the movie, her pulse began to pound. She rested her forehead against his shoulder.

"You are like a furnace."

When he laughed, she felt the vibrations under her cheek. His hand caressed her back as they lay together silently, watching the movie. She savored just being here with him, feeling his breath and his body against hers.

"I can't seem to stay away from you. I tried, but it is too hard."

"I can't promise you where this will go, Kyle."

Kissing her, he replied, "I am not asking you to." Right now, more than anything, she wished she could give this man her heart, but she was still stinging from Bennett's betrayal. Could she trust something that felt so natural, so easy? There had to be a catch somewhere.

- - - - - ● ● ● ● ● ● ● ● ● ● - - - -

As Kyle watched Lexi sleep, he finally realized that he wanted her because he loved her. The realization astonished him.

A part of him begged and pleaded with him to tell Lexi how he felt. But the timing was not right. He would be lost without her, and letting his feelings known may scare her away.

This woman had made an unforgettable mark on his life. The pain would be too much without her. He would go mad. For now, he would have to accept that they were friends, and friends only.

Chapter 33

The drive to Kyle's house was a pleasant one. The weather was perfect today. As the baby gave her a good sound kick, she stated, "We are almost there and then I can stretch."

She read somewhere that children learned to recognize their mother's voice while in the womb. Ever since then, she had talked to her baby as much as she could. She wanted this baby to know just how loved it was no matter what happened. This child would have a mother it could count on, even if Bennett had no plans on being a proper father.

If only she knew what Bennett intended to do. He recently said that he would try to make room for this child, but gave no guarantees. Seriously, try to make room for your child? Well, if that was the attitude he planned on taking, then they did not need him in their lives.

- -

A gentle breeze blew Lexi's hair across her cheek as she stood in the driveway beside her car. She could not take her eyes off the superbly built man cutting the lawn. She was not expecting to find him cutting the grass nor the exquisite house.

As he stepped off the lawnmower, perspiration molded his form-fitting T-shirt to his body and gave her a glance of the strong bronze chest that was underneath.

Closing her eyes, she took a deep tremulous breath, trying to steady her racing heart as he made his way to her parked car. The sight of him standing in front of her caused her heart to gallop once again. She could not take her eyes off the hard muscular man in front of her.

She grasped his extended hand and felt the heat radiating off of his body. Even dressed in jeans and a shirt, he was an inordinately attractive man. With his firm jaw and high cheekbones, this was the first time she had ever seen him look so rugged and capable of doing anything he tried, mowing down any obstacle in his way.

A deft kick from her baby reminded her that she was hardly a candidate for romance.

Concerned, he asked, "Are you all right? You look a little flushed."

She pulled in a bolstering breath, smelling fresh cut grass and the man in front of her, "I'm fine. I got a little overheated."

"I wasn't expecting you so soon. I wanted to get the grass cut before it got too late. Come on in and rest while I get cleaned up."

She followed his quick steps as he led her through the overwhelming house. She looked around as the sound of their footsteps bounced off the walls. The house screamed luxury from the gorgeous marble floors to the priceless pieces of artwork adorning the walls. She felt out of place here. What made her think that she could belong in his world?

As they walked through a set of oversized mahogany doors, she looked around the warm, inviting room and felt herself relaxing. Along one of the walls was a fireplace so large that she could literally walk inside of it. While it was the centerpiece of the room, it also added a touch of comfort. The lighting hidden in the ceiling made the room feel incredibly romantic.

"Can I get you something to drink?"

She shook her head and gave him a smile, "I'm fine, thank you though."

She walked over to a comfortable looking sofa and sank into the soft leather. Now she was thankful she had accepted his invitation to supper at his house. Being inside of his house reaffirmed that she could not tell him how she felt. It was better to keep the relationship strictly at a friendship level.

At that moment, the baby kicked inside of her, a swift one-two shot to her bladder that almost sent her rushing to the bathroom. Running a hand over her belly, she still could not believe how much her life had changed these last several months.

The baby responded to her soothing touch by kicking her even harder this time. At the rate this child kicked, she suspected that she may have a football player on her hands. She could not wait to meet this tiny thing in three months.

As the baby gave her bladder another kick, she went in search of a bathroom. While searching for the bathroom, she took in more of Kyle's house. All around her was sheer decadence. She finally found a guest bathroom and was taken back by its luxury. The baby's nursery could fit inside the large bathroom. If this was a guest bathroom, she could just imagine what the master bedroom looked like.

Her eyes gravitated to the large oval garden tub. Looking at the shower, she noticed that it had more jets than should be allowed. She could just imagine what they'd feel like against a tired body. She never considered herself a material girl, but she could get used to these luxuries.

On her way back to the living room, she realized that the house was bigger than she expected, and was quite surprised that it was this large. It was also tastefully decorated, but suited him.

Unable to stop herself, she walked into the kitchen and lost her breath. Now, this was a kitchen to cook in. The gourmet kitchen was a chef's dream. Catching her by complete surprise, Kyle asked from behind her, "Can I get you anything?"

Startled by his sudden presence, she jumped at the sound of his voice. The mere sight of him and her breath caught. His dark hair was still wet from the shower, and his jeans hugged his body.

As his liquid brown eyes roamed over her body, she felt herself grow warm with anticipation. She shook her head, telling herself that he did not see her in that way. He was purely a good friend. Besides, she did not belong in his world. He needed a debutante girlfriend, someone who fit in this world of his.

"A glass of water would be nice."

"Are you sure you don't want something else? I know you aren't drinking alcohol, but I do have a soda or I can fix a cup of coffee."

"Water is okay. I don't seem to be drinking enough of it anyway and have been forcing myself to drink it more."

Motioning toward a chair at the bar, he instructed her, "Well, sit down and rest."

As she sat down on one of the high stools, she watched him putter around the kitchen. It was nice to watch a man work in the kitchen. Bennett never helped out around the house; he felt that it was her responsibility. At first, she loved waiting on him hand and foot, but toward the end, that was getting old.

As he handed her a bottle of water, their fingers brushed against each other. Her hand tingled from the mere touch. With him standing this close to her, she could breathe in his clean masculine scent. She found herself trembling from having him so near her. She told herself that it had to be because of the pregnancy; it had her hormones in overdrive. She should put some distance between them; somewhere that she could not smell him or feel the heat of his body so close to her. Just being around him, she felt the vibrations of sexual energy that exuded from his body.

He asked, "Do you want to go out to eat or would you rather eat here?"

"Let's eat here. I've been dealing with cranky customers all day and just want to prop my feet up."

Smiling, he pulled her to her feet, "Well, I went ahead and downloaded a few movies for us to watch tonight. I can order Chinese or pizza if you'd like."

"Hmm, Chinese sounds good, but if you would rather a pizza, that is fine with me. I am easy."

"Chinese is fine by me. Do you want anything in particular?"

"Lately, I can eat anything, so it doesn't matter to me."

- - - - - - ● ● - - - - - - - -

He looked down at her growing stomach and smiled. She could no longer hide the fact that she would soon be a mother. He was proud of the way she handled this whole fiasco. Most women would have broken down long before now, but she still kept pushing forward. He doubted that her slimeball of an ex-husband was doing anything to help her along the way either. She had not said anything, but he had known Bennett long enough to know what he was like.

Unable to stop himself, he walked over to her and gathered her into his arms. He looked down at her startled; he felt the baby kick him as he molded her body to his.

She smiled up at him, "I guess the baby wants to thank you for the warm hug as well."

"I will be here for you Lexi. I just want you to know that." Even as he said the words, he knew that he wanted to do much more than that. He wanted to take care of this woman and the baby she was carrying.

He took a deep breath and tightened his arms around her, splaying one hand along her back. She felt like heaven in his arms. His body came alive as he breathed in her alluring scent. She smelled like a fresh summer day, reminiscent of freshly picked flowers with just a hint of honey. A warm smile formed on his handsome face as his other hand played with a few loose tendrils of hair fluttering against her face.

He wanted to make all of her problems go away. If he could banish Bennett from her life, he would, but he knew there may be a time when he was actually ready to step into his child's life.

He placed a hand on her stomach and gazed into her eyes. He smiled as the baby gave him a swift hard kick. "You may just have a football player on your hands."

"I have been saying the same thing. This child likes to kick up a storm."

He bent down and kissed her stomach. "I don't know about you, but I am hungry."

"I am always hungry lately."

- - - - - - - - ● - - - - - - - -

As she watched him warm up leftover pasta for them both, she thought about the path their relationship was now exploring. There was a connection between them that she had never shared with another man.

The only thing holding her back was doubt. She was not sure if she was ready to trust her heart to another man just yet.

Whenever she thought about Kyle, her heart skipped a beat. If only she were brave enough to give him her whole heart, to let love wrap her in its warm embrace. Perhaps, she should listen to everyone's advice and move on with her life. After all, Bennett surely had.

She needed to take back her life, especially with a baby on the way. She did not want a life full of regrets. If she wanted to take control of her life, she needed to be certain of what she was doing.

As if sensing her dark thoughts, Kyle walked over to her, tilted her head up to his and kissed her. What started out as a light kiss to help calm her nerves turned into a passionate kiss that neither of them wanted to end.

Chapter 34

Lexi walked out of her office and into the lobby and noticed Kyle waiting for her. Walking over to kiss him, she stated, "This is a surprise. To what do I owe this honor?"

Laughing as he took her by the hand, they walked out of the hotel lobby, "I thought I would treat you to supper. I figured we could grab a bite to eat together before taking you home."

"Mmmm, that sounds perfect. I am starving. I have thought about Little River Inn all afternoon and a large bowl of their gumbo." This particular restaurant became a favorite of hers as soon as they opened their doors. She could already taste the BBQ shrimp appetizer and their mouthwatering gumbo.

The drive to the restaurant was breathtaking with the glimmer of raindrops clinging to the trees, reluctant to fall into the puddles below. In front of them, there was a rainbow that gracefully arched across the sky.

This restaurant made its mark in Springport upon its grand opening. The food was transcendent. The chef delivered sophisticated flavors with skillfully composed plates from a menu that changed daily, using only ingredients that were in season.

As the waiter handed them their menus, Lexi looked over at Kyle and smiled.

He reached across from the small intimate table to take her hand in his. She could feel the heat emanating from his body. When she caught a whiff of his cologne, her pulse quickened. Every pore in her body was tingling, begging for his touch. Even his voice sent shivers down her spine. Listening to him speak sent erotic images of hot, sultry nights with the scent of jasmine heavy in the air.

A young woman appeared before them with a pad and pen in hand, "Hi, I'm Emma. Would y'all like something from the bar?"

Kyle looked up at her, "I would like a Manhattan made with Maker's Mark, please."

Lexi told her, "I will just have water."

The waitress asked, "Do y'all want an appetizer to start off with?"

Kyle nodded his head, "We would like an order of the BBQ shrimp."

"Very good, sir. Have you decided what you would like to eat or do you need a few more minutes?"

He perused the menu one more time, "I would like the Crawfish Acadian."

"Yes, sir, and you miss?"

Lexi handed her the menu, already knowing what she wanted. "I would like a bowl of your seafood gumbo, the house potato salad, and some of your homemade French bread, please."

"That's an excellent choice. I had a sample of the gumbo earlier, and it is delicious."

Lexi looked up at the waitress and smiled. She knew what she wanted before they even arrived. Even though there were so many wonderful dishes to choose from, she craved gumbo lately. She could live off of gumbo right now.

The waitress collected their menus, "I'll be right back with your drinks."

Lexi broke open one of the fresh rolls that the waitress had placed on the table and inhaled the aroma of fresh baked bread. While they waited for their food, they talked about their day.

As the waitress placed their appetizers on the table, she watched as the steam floated upwards and dissipated. Unable to resist the tempting aroma, she dove into the BBQ shrimp with sheer abandon.

The buttery sauce coated her tongue as the spices came alive in her mouth. The shrimp were plump and tender. She moaned in ecstasy as she ate. Unable to help herself, she broke off a piece of the fresh bread and dredged it into the rich butter.

They talked throughout dinner. As they walked back to the car, he placed his hand on the small of her back. Just this simple gesture meant so much to her. It made her feel special and protected.

As they pulled up to her house, Lexi looked over at Kyle, "Would you like to come in for a nightcap?"

"Are you sure you are up to company tonight? I know I sprang dinner on you and didn't know if you just wanted to go home and fall sound asleep."

Smiling over at him, she grabbed his hand to kiss it gently. "I would love it if you came inside for a nightcap."

- - - - - ● ●● ● ● ●●●● ● ●● ●● ● ● - - -

The next morning, Lexi found it difficult to focus on her work. She kept wondering if her feelings for Kyle were the real thing. She thought she truly loved Bennett and look where that landed her. Yet, when Kyle made love to her, it was more than physical attraction. She was convinced that love was present.

Whenever he looked at her, she not only felt desirable but special. He knew that she was carrying another man's child, but that did not seem to bother him; however, before the baby came into this world they had to discuss this. She needed to know that he had no problems with her giving birth to Bennett's child. The last thing she wanted was her child to bond with a man who would not be there for the long haul.

She needed to make sure that he had feelings for not only her, but also for her child. For goodness sake, she had not even asked him if he wanted to take on a fatherly role. Lord knew that Bennett wanted no part of his or her life.

Chapter 35

On the trip to the funeral home, Lexi shook her head in disbelief. It was still hard to believe that her ex-mother-in-law had died. She looked over at Christi, "I can't thank you enough for taking me."

Christi smiled over at her friend, "You know I would do anything for you, honey. I don't understand why you want to go to this funeral, though. The woman made your life a living nightmare, and her son was no better."

Lexi shrugged her shoulders, "I don't understand it myself. I guess I feel a responsibility to the baby. The woman was my child's grandmother after all."

Christi scoffed, "She never even acknowledged that you were carrying her grandchild. Besides, the woman was a royal bitch to you."

Lexi shuddered thinking about the hard times Marlene Daigle gave her. "I know. I still can't believe that she is dead. I thought evil incarnate could never actually die."

Christi laughed, "Perhaps the only thing that kept her alive was making your life miserable, and since you are out of Bennett's life, she had nothing to live for."

A frown furrowed Lexi's brow and she let out a long sigh, "She sure did her best to make my life miserable. What made things worse was Bennett never once stood up for me, but with April, it is an entirely different matter. Bennett's family has treated the woman like a princess."

"Yet, here we are getting ready to pay respect to a woman who never once showed you an ounce of respect."

"I know. Perhaps, I need to confirm that the woman is dead."

When Lexi first heard that Marlene Daigle had passed away, she thought good riddance, but there had also been a part of her that felt an overwhelming sadness. Perhaps, it was the pregnancy hormones causing her to act this way.

As they walked into the funeral home, she started to have second thoughts. Maybe she had not thought this through. Bennett would not treat her with any respect, and she said a quick prayer that he did not start a scene when he saw her.

As she looked down at Marlene's body, she once again contemplated why she had come. If it was for closure, it would not happen. It was not like the woman would pop up from the coffin and apologize for how she treated Lexi all these years. This woman had been the biggest bitch to walk this earth when it came to her.

She still found it hard to believe that Marlene's reign of terror had come to an end.

Christi whispered in Lexi's ear, "Bennett is headed this way."

Lexi rolled her eyes as the baby gave her a hard kick. She did not want a confrontation at his mother's funeral. She should not have come; seeing Bennett in this setting had emotions stabbing at her heart.

He must be taking better care of himself; he was starting to look like the man she fell in love with all those years ago. He had lost weight, and from the look of him, he had been hitting the tanning bed. His money situation must also be improving. He was wearing a pair of slacks and coat that appeared to be custom made. Even his tie looked expensive with its funky, trendy print, more than likely something April picked out for him.

As she was leaving the funeral home before Bennett could reach her, she pushed away a wishful vision of him in a coffin right next to his mother. She stifled a giggle as she looked at Christi. If she knew what Lexi was thinking, she would help her concoct a plan to make that very thing happen.

Before Lexi escaped to the outside, a hand grabbed her shoulder, "What are you doing here?"

Lexi jumped at the harshness in his voice. Swallowing down a sarcastic remark, Lexi stated, "Bennett, I am so sorry about your mother."

As he gripped her shoulder even tighter, Lexi felt self-conscious under his gaze, "You aren't welcome here Lexi." Jabbing a finger at her stomach, he stated, "The last thing April needs is to see you and…and…and this here. Unlike you, she loved my mother and her death has April devastated."

Her throat constricted, and she averted her eyes to keep him from seeing how his venomous remarks affected her. The last thing she wanted to do was give him the pleasure of knowing that his remarks did hurt her.

Before Bennett could jab at her belly once again, Kyle rushed to Lexi's side and grabbed Bennett's finger. "Bennett, I think that's enough of you tormenting Lexi. You have no reason to be so rough with her. After all, she is carrying your child."

Bennett sneered at Lexi, "What? You have him coming to your rescue now?" Glaring at Kyle, he said, "You are supposed to be my friend. You should be here paying condolences and not coming to her rescue. Besides, I don't even know if that baby is mine. Lord knows she was never home enough to pay me any real attention when we were married. For all I know, when she was 'working' she could have been banging another man."

Looking at his friend with burning hatred, "Maybe she had an affair with you."

Kyle released the man's finger, and commented snidely, "Bennett, you should know better than that. Lexi would never cheat on you. She thought you hung the moon."

Lexi exclaimed, "Besides, you have no room to talk. Exactly when did you start banging other women, after we were married or before?"

Bennett looked at her with a malicious grin, "Well, perhaps if you had been a better wife, I wouldn't have sought comfort with other women. Instead, you were more concerned with your career."

Before the conversation could get even more heated, Kyle interjected, "Lexi, let Christi take you home."

Christi pulled Lexi out the door, "Come on Lexi; let's go." Christi turned back to Bennett, "She is a better woman than me. I'd have waited until the woman was six feet under and came back to dance on her grave singing ding dong the witch is dead, at the top of my lungs."

Lexi giggled at the vision of Christi dancing and singing on the old harpy's grave. Pulling Christi outside, "Now why didn't I think of that earlier? We could have had a party. I'm sure a number of people would have come."

Once Kyle, Christi, and Lexi were back in Lexi's house, Christi stated, "Did either of you notice that Bennett didn't appear to be upset about his mother's death?"

Kyle looked at the two women, "I did some investigating into a few things, such as why Bennett was harping for Lexi to have an abortion. It appears that he owes the wrong people a vast amount of money. If he wants to continue living here, or even living, he has to pay up."

Lexi looked over at Kyle with surprise in her eyes, "What do you mean he owes the wrong people money?"

"Well, it turns out he has done a lot of gambling. He owes numerous bookies and loan sharks money."

Lexi could feel the anger toward Bennett building up once more, "So, let me get this straight, not only was the bastard screwing women and using my money to pay for his trysts during our marriage, but he was also throwing our money out the window by gambling?"

Christi took Lexi's hand in hers, "Girl, consider yourself lucky to be rid of him. You are free from that son of a biscuit eater!"

Chapter 36

Lexi took a deep breath and let the aroma of Christmas overtake her. The fragrances of peppermint and hot chocolate mixed with the smell of spruce trees. In town, shoppers chatted as they gathered around the edges of shops, pointing to the display windows full of sparkly packages and Christmas trees, while others bustled by with smiling faces, despite the cumbersome bags they carried. The town had Christmas music playing in the background.

Lexi found herself excited about this Christmas. Although money would be tight, she found herself in an impulsive gift giving mood.

Even the guests that stayed at the hotel recently seemed to be full of the Christmas spirit. They seemed to have joy on their faces, and in a festive mood. Even though she was in the holiday mood, she could feel the tension in her back. She despised that Bennett still refused to acknowledge his child. A part of her was hoping for some Christmas magic to make things change.

Lexi made her way gingerly across the street and entered the coffee shop. The glass dessert case had its shelves full of miniature cakes and cookies. There were also a few Christmas novels displayed on some nearby tables for reading.

This small café was teeming with chattering customers who would burst into rounds of laughter. Several held shopping bags in various shades of red and green, their joviality jarring her with feelings. On the counter was a pedestal holding cookies frosted in a Christmas theme. There were also cupcakes available in vanilla and chocolate with white icing and sprinkles. There were so many tempting treats to choose from, and Lexi was unsure of what she wanted to go with her coffee.

This little café was the epitome of charm. It had wavy glass, double bay windows that they used for display. There was a small sitting area that had a comfortable sofa and a few padded chairs where customers could get a cup of coffee and a specialty pastry and read for a little while.

Lexi took a step behind the person in line, her attention on the coffee choices. Once she settled on something, Lexi dug around in her purse for her money.

Lexi ordered her a white chocolate latte, handed the barista her money and waited for her order. As Lexi waited for her order, she looked around at the Christmas decorations and the tree in the corner. She was hoping that Christmas would help improve her mood.

- - - - - - - - - ● - - - - - - - - -

Lexi pulled into the driveway of her parents' house. The large brick colonial was a display with Christmas lights, the tree twinkling in the front window. The front porch had greenery spiraling up the poles, with a bright red Christmas bow at the top and with the ribbon cascading down toward the ground. One of

Lexi's favorite traditions had always been decorating the house for Christmas.

Lexi walked inside and headed toward the kitchen. "Mom, I hope you didn't start making cookies without me?"

Lexi's mom came rushing out of the kitchen, "I didn't hear you come in. Of course, I didn't start making cookies without you." Lexi gave her a quick smile and her mom kissed the top of her head.

In the kitchen, her mom had a candle burning, one that reminded her of warm cinnamon spice tea, and Christmas music playing from the small CD player. On the kitchen counter, she had all the ingredients out to make the various traditional Christmas cookies they would bake.

Lexi rubbed her stomach and smiled, "I can't wait for this little one to be able to help us. It will be so much fun."

Lexi's mom asked her, "Did you want to make the gingerbread cookies first, or the sugar cookies?"

"How about the English teacakes?"

"Those were always your favorite."

As Lexi looked around the house, she realized how quiet it was, "Where is Dad at?"

"He went to get some more firewood. The temperature is supposed to drop tonight, and it's going to get cold."

Before they could continue the conversation, Janie walked in with Grant and Madison, "Sorry we're late, I hope we didn't miss any of the fun."

Lexi told her, "You're just in time. We are about to start making English teacakes."

Grant whined, "Ah, I was hoping we can make sugar cookies first."

Lexi giggled, "Well, then, I guess I can let you have your way. We can make sugar cookies first."

Over the next few hours, the family laughed, prepared and baked cookies, and enjoyed their time together.

The festivities brought an air of excitement to the house.

Chapter 37

By the seventh month, Lexi's belly had grown much larger, and her energy levels were depleting fast. Whoever wrote those pregnancy books did not gather all the relevant information. Everything she had read said she should be glowing and bursting with energy. That was such a pack of lies. It took everything she had to make it through the day and drag herself home at night.

To make matters worse, she still had not started to get anything for the nursery or the baby. She decided to decorate the room in a pretty green, one that was not quite minty green or a bright neon green, but right in the middle. She still needed to pick out the furniture and buy a few clothes for when the baby was born.

Right now, she felt lost. She had so many things that needed to be done. Bennett still took every chance he could to convince her that he did not want to see this child born. At times Lexi was frightened of him, particularly when she saw that look of pure hatred in his eyes. She had not seen him like this before. She had never suspected that Bennett would harm a hair on her head or a child about to be born, but now, she was not so sure.

Her mom and dad offered to let her stay there after the baby was born for her to recover and adjust to motherhood, but that would not work either. Her mom was still hanging on to some ridiculous fantasy that the baby's birth would have Bennett coming around and wanting to get back together. She never told her family that Bennett had been pressuring her to end the pregnancy or put the baby up for adoption. Besides, even if Bennett did come crawling back on his hands and knees, she would not take him back.

That night as soon as she got home, she fixed herself a large tub of hot water to soak in. While the water ran, she added some new bubble bath she found at a small boutique called "Voodoo Moon". She fell in love with the provocative scent instantly; it reminded her of being in love. But she may have wasted her money. She certainly could not seduce a man right now. Not only was her belly getting bigger, but so was her derriere.

As the tub finished filling, she undressed and climbed in. As the water enveloped her with its warmth, she felt her muscles relaxing. The heat of the water seemed to help erase all her aches and pains. She rubbed her hands along her belly as the baby continued to play a game of football with her bladder.

As she breathed in the scent of the bubble bath, she calmed her mind and body. She had no plans of leaving this tub until the water grew cold. She was in heaven and closed her eyes.

When the water cooled, she got out the tub and wrapped herself in an oversized, fluffy green towel. Once dried, she rubbed the new lotion into her skin. The lady told her that this particular brand had a special combination of oils that would help keep her skin soft and minimize the stretch marks. She slipped on a pair of oversized knit shorts and a T-shirt; she may as well be comfortable.

While lying in bed, she pulled up a website that had a variety of baby items for sale. As she looked over the cribs that they had, the baby gave her a flurry of kicks. Laughing, she rubbed her stomach, "Are you trying to tell me that you like this crib little one?"

Her phone let out a loud beep, notifying her that she had a text message. She smiled when she saw that it was from Kyle, "Are you still awake?"

Instantly, she replied, "I am playing on the internet, looking at a few baby items."

"Open your door."

Smiling to herself, she wondered what he was up to. Climbing out of bed, she went to let him in. As soon as she opened the door, he swept her into his arms. She drew in a deep breath, catching a heady scent of his rich maleness. She parted her lips and met his devouring kiss.

She quickly pulled him inside, "What are you smiling at?"

"You. How beautiful you look."

Lexi rolled her eyes, "You're crazy. I'm fat. Hideous looking."

"No. You are not fat. You are pregnant, expecting a baby. There's a difference. And it is you. Who you are, what you look like, it's all you."

As she stood there near him, time was suspended. The outside world ceased to exist. It was only the two of them.

Chapter 38

Lexi woke up feeling out of sorts. After dressing for work, she walked slowly to the kitchen and began to prepare breakfast. Only nothing appealed. She settled for dry toast and tea.

Once at work, the uneasy feelings continued.
Lexi and Kyle were on their way back to her house from supper when a sudden pain struck her in the abdomen, so intense it caught her breath. Stunned, she held her stomach, trying to breathe through the pain. She could not be going into labor. It was far too soon. She was not close to term. But the gripping pain encircled her back and lower abdomen.

She took a deep breath and then another. Another sharp pain hit her, starting at her back and moving towards the front, low down and hard. She had to bite her bottom lip to keep from screaming.

She grabbed Kyle's arm, "I think you had better turn around."
He looked at her and saw her pale face. Concern for her well being rushed over him as he panicked, "Lexi, you don't look good."

Before she could answer, another sharp pain gripped low in her stomach. Before she recovered from that pain there came more.

Once the pains subsided, she told him, "We need to get to the hospital. I think I am in labor."

"Wait, what? You aren't due for what at least another month?"

She was not sure if this was labor, but she was concerned for the welfare of her baby. She needed to make sure that this was not premature labor. "I have another five weeks to go." She confessed, "I'm having sharp pains, but there is no way this is labor. It's not time! What if something is wrong with the baby? Ow..." She panicked when another sharp pain struck. Lexi held back the tears, "Kyle, I can't lose this baby. I'm so afraid."

As they walked through the emergency room doors, Lexi gripped his arms hard. Suddenly, she felt lightheaded. Using him for support, she closed her eyes and waited for the room to settle.

"Lexi, what's wrong? Do you need me to get you a wheelchair?"

"I'm just dizzy all of a sudden."

Before they could move another step, another pain gripped her stomach, this one worse than the others. She almost doubled over as she clutched her stomach. She clamped her jaws and waited for the pain to pass.

Thankfully, a nurse was returning to her desk when she saw Lexi and Kyle. She grabbed a wheelchair, and pushed it over to where they were standing. "Come on honey. Let's get you admitted so a doctor can take a look at you."

By the time the nurse had her on the exam table, the pain had intensified. If only she had started the childbirth classes early. She kept telling herself that she had plenty of time. Now, here she was in the hospital with no clue as to what she should do.

As her breathing became even heavier, the nurse asked Kyle, "Have you and your wife gone to the Lamaze classes yet?"

He looked at her, then the nurse and back again in confusion. Lexi informed the nurse through clenched teeth, "I haven't started the classes yet. I thought I still had at least five weeks."

"Hmm, okay. Well, let's get the doctor in here and make sure you are in labor."

The nurse looked at Kyle and told him, "I hope that you are at least planning on staying here with her. It is good to have fathers involved with the whole birthing process. It has been proven that when fathers aid in bringing their child into the world an instant bonding takes place. Besides, she will need a strong hand when the hard labor starts."

Lexi started to tell the nurse, "You don't understand…" but was stopped short when another excruciating pain cut across her lower abdomen before she could explain that Kyle was not the baby's daddy, but here to offer moral support.

Lexi prayed that the doctor arrived soon. It was way too early for her baby to be born. Just then, a knock sounded at the door, and Dr. Allen walked in the room. "Well then, I hear we have a baby trying to make its debut."

As he examined her, he confirmed her fears, "Well, it isn't Braxton Hicks contractions. You are indeed in early labor."

Lexi squeezed Kyle's hand for comfort as she tried to fight back the tears threatening to spill. He asked Dr. Allen, "Is there any way to stop the contractions?"

"I will try to stop the labor. Lexi's contractions are causing her cervix to open earlier than normal, but her membranes are still intact. If we can get her rehydrated, that should help stop the labor."

A fetal monitor was hooked up to monitor the baby's vitals.

Looking at Lexi, he scolded her, "I warned you at your last appointment to slow down. You aren't doing you or the baby any good working around the clock."

Kyle looked at her with a new determination in his eyes, "I will make sure that she listens to every order you give her Dr. Allen. Even if that means I have to chain her to a bed."

"Well, depending on how today goes; you may have to do that. If the early labor keeps up, she will need to stay in bed with her legs propped up."

As he was talking, the nurse came in with an IV bag. Dr. Allen told Lexi, "We will start you on an IV of magnesium sulfate. In most cases, rehydrating the mother and keeping her on her side for a particular period of time is enough to stop premature labor." Looking over at Kyle, he told him, "She will be here for several hours."

Still holding Lexi's hand Kyle replied, "I am not going anywhere."

Dr. Allen told Lexi, "It is important that we stop the premature labor. The longer the baby stays in the womb, the less chance there is for the child to have neurological and other health problems. I want to do an ultrasound and see how developed your baby's lungs are." Looking her directly in the eyes, "You may have to be put on bed rest until the baby is born. We will know more in a few hours."

Lexi groaned, "I can't just stay in bed. I have to work. If I lose my job, I also lose my health insurance."

Kyle looked at Lexi, "You and the baby are more important than work."

Lexi just looked at him. Just when she thought her life was looking up, she felt as if her world was crumbling down around her once more. "If I have to stay in bed for the remainder of my pregnancy, I can stay at the hotel. At least then I can keep an eye on things and get some work done."

Dr. Allen looked at Lexi, "That isn't what I meant when I said to take it easy. However, if you can promise me that you will take it easy, I will grant you that request."

Before she could answer, Kyle responded, "I will make sure that she listens to you, Dr. Allen." Kyle looked at Lexi, "Why don't you just stay at my house? That way I can make sure your needs are tended to."

Lexi shook her head, "You are already doing more than enough by just being here for me. I don't want to put you out."

Sensing she was going to be stubborn, Kyle picked up his phone, "Well then, I guess I should call your parents and let them know what is going on. Knowing your mom, she will insist that you move back home until the baby is born. I'm sure that she will want you to stay there for a few weeks after the baby's birth as well."

Lexi gasped, "You wouldn't call my mom. She is already trying everything in her power to get me and

Bennett back together. This will be the ammunition that she needs to try and convince me to take Bennett back. Even Bennett attempted to tell her that he is happy with April."

Smiling Kyle said, "So then, what will it be?"

"I will take you up on your offer and stay a few days at your house."

"I knew you would see it my way."

"I don't know what I would do without you. There are not many men who would even bother with a woman carrying another man's baby."

Over the years he had become content with his quiet life, but the idea of sharing a home with her-even for a few days-had him excited.

As he looked at Lexi, he wondered if he could find the courage to tell her what his real motive was. "I want to make sure that you and the baby are okay. I will make sure that you are well taken care of, and the baby is born healthy."

Over the next several hours, the contractions slowed, grew less severe and finally stopped.

Chapter 39

Feeling better the next day, Lexi decided it would not hurt to slip away to the hotel for a quick visit.

"Lexi, why are you here?" Mr. Devonshire asked when he saw her at the front desk.

"I had some work that needed to be done."

"Does your doctor know that you are here? I thought Kyle said you needed to take it easy."

"I'm okay. I really need to get this work done. Besides, most women work until their due date."

"Well, if you ask me, you look exhausted. And you were just in the hospital. You should be taking it easy." He looked over at her, "How many months are you now?"

"I still have at least another five weeks before the baby is born. I'm fine."

She could tell that her boss wanted to argue more, so she informed him, "I'm not going to stay here long. I just want to get some things done and then I will go home and put my feet up."

"If you start feeling contractions, tired, anything out of the ordinary, please let us know."

Looking down at the floor and shuffling his feet, he asked, "Have you decided what you're going to do once the baby is born?"

"I was going to talk to you about that. My office is big enough where I can keep the baby in a playpen while at work."

Sighing, he informed Lexi, "I don't think this is the right atmosphere to let your baby stay in while you work." He looked at Lexi, "I will allow you to bring the baby in until you have found a suitable daycare, and I understand occasionally there will be times the child needs to be here. However, it is not the place a child needs to stay at every day. Too much can go wrong."

Lexi could feel her heart breaking. She had thought it would be easy to convince him to allow her to keep the baby here. Now, what was she going to do? She feared her salary would not be enough to afford a daycare close to here. Especially one that met her criteria.

The fear of losing her job made her blood turn cold. She had worked too hard to earn this job.

Panic washed over her. How was she going to cope? The impossibility of it all became overwhelming. She willed herself to be calm and slow her racing mind. But that did not help.

Chapter 40

Lexi had been at Kyle's house for only three days, and she was already going stir crazy. She was not sure if she could do this whole bed rest thing, she was about ready to pull out her hair. She lost count of how many books she'd read on her eBook reader and watched umpteen movies, but she was still bored out of her mind.

A knock at the living room door surprised her. As she heard the voice getting closer, she groaned. "Mom, what brings you here?"

"I wanted to see how you and the baby are doing."

After her mother gave her a cursory kiss on the cheek, she settled in a chair across from Lexi. "I am doing okay. The preterm labor has stopped. I have another doctor's appointment in two days. I hope that he will let me go back to work if I promise to take it easy."

Her mother looked at her intently, "Have you called Bennett and told him what is going on?"

"Mom, Bennett has no interest in this pregnancy or this child. He has a new wife and baby on the way. That is where he is putting all of his interest."

"Well, I don't see how he can be so inconsiderate. This is his baby, too."

Lexi shrugged her shoulders, "I'm not sure Mom. It will be okay though. This baby will be well loved."

"What about Bennett's dad?   Has he shown any interest in his new grandbaby?"

"You know his parents never liked me. His father and Bennett are doting on April so much that I don't think they even take this baby into consideration."

Her mom let out a deep sigh, "You know, it will be hard to raise a child on your own. You can put the baby up for adoption."

Lexi looked at her mom, astonished that she would even suggest such a thing, "While I have nothing against adoption, I plan on raising this baby on my own."

"Well, I think Bennett is foolish." That was something Lexi could agree on with her mother. Lexi's mother continued, "There are ramifications to raising a child on your own. You will play both mother and father. You won't have anyone here to help you with midnight feedings and diaper changes."

Lexi looked over at her mother, "I am not the first woman to raise a child on her own, and I won't be the last. I know it will be hard, but I can do it."

"It will be hard finding a man who wants to date a woman with a child."

Lexi shrugged her shoulders, "I am sure there are plenty of men willing to raise another man's child. However, I am not ready to give my heart to another man. It will be hard for me to trust again after what Bennett has done."

- - - - - - - - ● - - - - - - - - - -

Kyle was getting ready to walk into the room when he overheard Lexi's conversation with her mother. His heart dropped, this was what he feared. Now, if he could get Lexi to change her mind.

Chapter 41

The next day, Kyle still could not take his mind off the conversation Lexi had with her mother. With Lexi, he had given her his heart and soul. He wanted to tell her how he felt, but he was not sure if he could put his feelings into words.

This woman was so different from any other woman he had dated. Perhaps, that was why his prior relationships failed; he had compared them to her. Other women saw him for his money, and they tried a little too hard to get his attention.

For as long as he had known Lexi, he suspected that there were facets to her that he may never discover. However, he wanted to spend his entire life trying to. Sex with Lexi was better than he imagined, but with her, it was much more than sex. With her, the barriers he built around himself had crumbled. It was just him and Lexi, heart to heart and soul to soul. He never knew what people meant when they said they loved someone with all of their heart but now he did.

Now that he knew that he wanted to spend his life with her, he had to know for certain, "Lexi, can you answer a question honestly?"

As he contemplated asking her what he must, he captured her hand, rubbing the pad of his thumb along the inside of her wrist. The subtle movement sent a spark of desire straight through her body, "Will you ever be able to trust your heart to another man?"

Lexi let out a deep sigh, "I'd like to think so. I pray that I will eventually move on."

"What if a man wants to be more than just friends?"

- - - - - - ●● ● ●● - - - - - - - -

Lexi looked at Kyle, wondering why he asked such questions. She had him pegged as a man afraid of commitment. She always thought of him as a man looking for hot sex with no strings. Even though they had shared intimate, passion filled nights; she never let herself believe that he saw her as wife material. Besides, she was carrying his friend's child. She did not see him as one of those men willing to raise another man's child.

"Before I fall in love with a man, I want to make sure he won't abuse my heart. When I say 'I do' again, it will be forever. I want to grow old with my husband. I want to make sure my next husband won't betray me the way Bennett did. More importantly, he has to love this child as much as he would love his own child."

"How can a man prove that you are the love of his life?"

She picked up her glass and swirled the tea around. As she watched the amber liquid and ice swirl together, she thought deeply about his question. Would she consider dating again? Probably not right now. She liked the arrangement they had, but to date someone exclusively at this point in her life was not what she had in mind. Besides, dating could lead to emotions that she was not ready for. Dating could also lead to heartbreak, and she'd had enough of that.

When she looked back up at him, the look in his eyes had her heart skipping a beat. There was a hunger there that she did not notice earlier. It sent a shock of excitement straight to her heart.

As she continued to look into his eyes, the rest of her surroundings seemed to melt away. She could imagine running her hands over every square inch of his hot, purely male body. Swallowing down the desire that bubbled to the surface, she told him, "To be honest, I haven't given it a lot of thought lately." Running her hand over her stomach, "Besides, it's not like I am the greatest catch right now. I don't have men panting after me."

He looked her body up and down. "I think you are wrong. You are a beautiful woman, especially now."

"You have to say that. You are my best friend."

He took her hand in his and kissed it gently, "You are a gorgeous woman. Bennett was a fool. You deserve far better than that. Any guy would be lucky to fall in love with you. You can't let what Bennett did turn you off of all men for good." Leaning into her, he took a strand of her hair and tucked it behind her ear, "I have never met a woman like you. You are stronger than you realize."

Her stomach fluttered as she listened to his words. What would he say if he learned of all the doubts she had about herself? Her self-confidence was nonexistent. "Kyle, you have no idea how much I value your friendship. You have been here for me throughout this whole ordeal. You even agreed to be there with me for the birth of the baby, which I know must scare the hell out of you, yet, you agreed to do it. I could not have made it through any of this without you. I also respect your opinion. Eventually, I may get back on the horse and try to date again, but that terrifies me. You are the only person in this whole world who understands me. What if I never find a man who cares for me as I am, warts and all?"

- - - - - - - - ● - - - - - - - - -

Kyle groaned in his mind. This was not going the way he expected it to. He had hoped that Lexi would hear his words and realize that he was falling madly in love with her and jump straight into his arms. That did not appear to be the case though. However, sensing tonight was not the time to bring up his undying love for her, he backed off. He might try this conversation again later. For now, he had to be satisfied with things the way they were.

"You are a good woman and deserve a good man." He held off telling her that he believed he could be that man. He would ask her to marry him if she gave him the chance.

If he had read her expression right, he was moving too fast. She was not ready to move on just yet. He could tell by looking into her eyes that she still was not over the hate she had for Bennett. It was still too fresh for her.

- - - - - ● ● ● ● ● - - - - - -

Lexi wished she had the self-confidence to tell him she wanted to have him in her life. Yet, if she could not keep a man like Bennett interested in her, how could she ever hope to get a man like Kyle to stay with her for life?

Chapter 42

Needing some motherly advice, Kyle called his mom, "Do you feel like meeting for a cup of coffee?"

"I would love to, dear."

Half an hour later, Kyle met his mom at the café. He looked at his mom from across the table at the café and grimaced. "Okay, Kyle, spill it. Why did you want to meet for coffee this afternoon?"

"Can't a son want to see his mom?"

She took a sip of her latte and looked at him over the rim of the cup, "I know you. Something has been troubling you - now out with it."

He took in a deep breath, "I am in love with Lexi." There he said it - out loud.

A smile crept across her face. "Now, see, that wasn't so hard, was it."

He gave her a shocked look, "You know?"

"Oh honey, I have known for some time now. So what are you going to do about it?"

"What can I do? Bennett hurt her terribly."

"Show her that you are not Bennett and that you love her."

- - - - - ● ● ● ● ● ● ● ● ● ● ● - - - -

As they were headed to bed, Kyle gently kissed Lexi good night. He wanted so much more than this kiss, but he had to stop himself. However, when it came to Lexi, he found it hard to restrain himself. He constantly wanted more.

Every time she looked at him, his control hung on by a mere thread. As she walked away from him, she stopped and gasped. She turned around and looked at him, "You want to feel something amazing before going to sleep?"

That was a loaded question if he ever heard one. She took his hand and placed it on the side of her belly. He almost pulled back, reluctant to touch her, but she pressed his hand beneath her hand.

"Wait. You'll feel it."

A few seconds later, he felt a definite thump under his palm. He gave her a curious look, "The baby is really active tonight."

"Yep. Don't move just yet."

There were two more movements, almost like waves pushed against his hand. Some days he found it hard to believe that a living thing was inside her. A miracle. "I still don't see how it doesn't hurt when the baby kicks you."

"But it doesn't. It's sort of strange, almost like gas." They both laughed. After a few minutes, the movement stopped, "I guess he's asleep now."

Excitement showed in his eyes, "Do you know if it's a boy?"

"No. I told the doctor I wanted to be surprised, that I did not want to know."

As much as he wanted to continue standing here with Lexi, he knew he had to break it off. They had shared something special, but it did not change things. She did not belong to him, and it was not his baby.

"I guess I will call it a night. Good night Lexi, and sweet dreams."

Chapter 43

Kyle came into the living room and asked, "Lexi, would you mind if my mother joined us for supper tonight. She has been rather insistent lately about stopping by and checking in on you."

Lexi could feel the butterflies in her stomach, "No, that's fine. After all, this is your house." Lexi attempted to calm her nerves, "Would you like me to cook something for supper?"

"No, I don't want you stressing. I will call and order takeout so that we can take it easy today and enjoy our meal together."

At six o'clock that night, Kyle arrived home with supper and thirty minutes later his mom arrived. "Mrs. DuPont, it is so nice to see you again."

Kyle's mother gave her a warm hug, "My dear, it is so good to see you again." Stepping back and surveying Lexi she said, "And, you, my dear I wish I had looked that beautiful when I was pregnant with Kyle."

Lexi blushed, "I feel like a swollen blimp, but thank you for the compliment."

"Well, I don't know about you," she said, "but I am starving. Let's go in the dining room so we can eat and chat."

They passed around the platters of food. With a warm tone to her voice, Kyle's mother asked, "I know Kyle told me that they want you bedridden, but do you think it would be possible for us to have a small girls' day out? I would love to pamper you. I never had a daughter, and I think it would be fun to do. We can go get our hair done and we can have our nails done too."

From across the table, Kyle gave Lexi a look that told her she should graciously accept the offer. "I would be honored."

Kyle looked at his dinner guests, "Ladies, if you will excuse me, I will go get dessert."

Lexi smirked and asked, "Does it have chocolate?"

With a gleam in his eye, he teased, "Maybe, you have to wait and see."

As he left the room, Kyle's mother looked Lexi in the eyes, "My son loves you, you know. I have never seen him so happy. The look on his face when he sees you is priceless. You can hear it in his voice when he talks about you."

Lexi shook her head, "No, we are just friends. Besides, it would not be right for me to expect him to raise his best friend's baby."

"Pish posh, dear. That man loves you and the baby is part of you. He would love it like it was his own."

Was she right? Did Kyle love her?

Lexi lay in bed thinking about everything Kyle's mom had said.

Rolling off the edge of the bed, she sat up. Perhaps a swim would help relax her, put her to sleep. In the bathroom, she put on her swimsuit, and headed to the pool.

The luxurious pool had been a godsend. It gave her exercise without too much strain. Hopefully tonight it would relax her so that she could have a night of uninterrupted sleep.

Lexi spent the following day with Kyle's mother. They went to the hairdresser, had a facial, and even manicures and pedicures. As they enjoyed their pampering, she told Lexi about some of the pranks Kyle played growing up.

As the day progressed, Lexi found herself wishing that her ex-mother-in-law would have shown one-tenth of this type of kindness to Lexi. Instead, it was as if it was her daily mission to make Lexi's life a living nightmare.

Chapter 44

Lexi was tired of staying still. She needed to do something other than lay around. Then it hit her; she would cook Kyle supper. Besides, she needed to practice her cooking skills, and with a kitchen like he had, it would be a pure joy to cook.

As she looked over the recipe once more, she checked the ingredients she had lined up on the island. It looked as if she did indeed have everything she needed to make the shrimp étouffée. She was surprised to see how well stocked Kyle kept his pantry, fridge, and freezer. She was beginning to think that this man had a secret passion that he kept hidden from her. Of course, with him working on the water as he did, it would only make sense that he kept his freezer full of fresh seafood. There was such a good selection of seafood in the freezer that she had a hard time choosing what to cook. She knew that shrimp would not take long to defrost, plus, it had been a while since she had a shrimp étouffée. Unfortunately, this would be her first time to cook it, and she prayed it would be edible.

After she put the rice to cook, she started with the rest of the meal and lost herself in the joy of cooking and hummed to herself while she cooked.

A voice from behind startled her, "Well, it looks as if someone is having a good time."

"Your kitchen is amazing. I was going stir crazy and couldn't resist coming in here to play."

As he moved into the kitchen, he rolled up his sleeves. "Can I help you with anything?"

"From the look of this kitchen and the food that you have stocked, you must really enjoy cooking."

"I like to experiment with recipes."

He walked over to the stove and smelled the aromas rising from the pots, "Mmmm, I must admit that it smells good."

"Hopefully it tastes as good as it smells. I hope you don't mind, but I defrosted some shrimp for an étouffée. Keep your fingers crossed that I didn't ruin two pounds of the prettiest shrimp that I have ever seen."

"A lot of the shrimpers and fishermen on the wharfs like to trade. If I come in with extra fish, they will trade some of their catch."

She smiled over at him, "You enjoy your new job, don't you?"

Nodding his head, he admitted, "I enjoy running the fishing charters. Not only do you meet a variety of clients, but it is nice being out there on the water. I am considering working on getting my captain's license so that I can drive the boats as well. I am already contemplating adding another boat to the company. I have a thirty-foot Osprey Pilothouse Long Cabin, but a gentleman at the dock has a forty-five foot Viking, which can be used for sport fishing. He has some financial problems and wants to get out from underneath some of his debts."

"A lot of people are still suffering in this economy."

Nodding his head, he stated, "I know. I feel guilty moving in on someone else's misfortune, but there is no way I can make this business work if I pay full price for a boat."

"You are being sensible in your business dealings. My dad always stressed to us that it was wise to buy second hand and let some other sucker take the hit for the loss."

She swiped her hands together before smiling over at him, "Okay, I hope you are hungry. Everything is ready. Where do you want to eat?"

"Since you went to all this trouble, we should sit in the dining room."

After they had fixed their plates, they moved into the dining room. As they enjoyed their meal, they talked about their day. She dreaded moving back home; she found it homey living here with him. It was almost as if they were a happy family.

She watched as he seemed to enjoy his meal, savoring each mouthful. She had to admit that it was delicious; her cooking skills were improving.

After supper, he insisted on her relaxing while he cleaned up the dishes. Not wanting to part from his company, she sat at the bar and continued talking to him while he finished up with the dishes.

Once finished, he asked, "Would you care to watch a movie or are you too tired?"

"Movie and popcorn sound perfect."

- - - - - - - - - ● - - - - - - - - -

Kyle continued to steal looks at Lexi rather than watching the movie. He had never seen Lexi look so beautiful. She was not wearing any makeup. Her fair skin and long, dark eyelashes stood out in dramatic contrast to her piercing eyes.

As she watched, he could see every emotion play openly on her beautiful face. Near the end of it, she fell sound asleep. The spaghetti strap on the tank top she changed into right before getting comfortable had slipped, giving him a glimpse of her full breast. His breath caught. Even though the clothes were not form fitting, he could still see the outline of her body which brought a quick rush of desire to him.

The woman lying next to him deserved warmth, tenderness, and love. If only she saw that he could give her that and so much more. He carefully gathered her into his arms, and she instinctively snuggled closer and placed her head on his chest.

He inhaled deeply, taking in her intoxicating smell. He felt her heart beat against his chest.

These last days having her in his house had been the happiest days ever. Without waking her up, he carried the woman he had fallen madly in love with to the bedroom.

- - - - - - ● ● ● ● ● ● ● ● - - - -

As the days blended into each other, Lexi and Kyle fell into a pattern. Lexi anxiously awaited Kyle's return from work. Once home, they cooked supper together and afterward, they moved into the study and each caught up on work. She missed being at the hotel, but if she were there in person, she would miss being here with Kyle.

She never noticed just how hard Kyle worked. Most mornings he left before sunrise, and once home, he tended to work in his study on the computer for a bit. She never realized how much work went into running a fishing charter. You had to keep up with advertising, promotions, attracting new clientele, as well as making sure your present clientele was pleased.

She also found it relaxing to take a swim before bed. The cool water from the pool helped dampen the hormones raging inside of her. True to his word, Kyle kept his hands to himself, but it was hard to keep her mind from wandering. Her body came alive whenever he was near.

Tonight as she sat across from him at supper, she looked into his eyes and read the fire burning in them.

As he continued to gaze into her eyes, she felt herself becoming the kindling in his firestorm. She was dizzy with excitement.

- - - - - - - ●● ● ●● - - - - - - -

Kyle could not take his eyes off of Lexi tonight. He enjoyed their lively, intelligent conversations. If only he could tell her that he loved her. However, if he told her how he felt, would she tell him she felt the same way?

As if sensing what he was thinking, she looked at him. He felt as if someone punched him in the stomach as the heat of her gaze seared him. He had to kiss her before he went crazy with want.

He walked over to where she sat and pulled her into his arms. His hands swept through her hair as his mouth devoured hers. He felt his pent-up frustration melt away.

He kissed every inch of her mouth as her hands moved through his hair. Her touch brought him dangerously close to the boiling point. He was no longer in control of his emotions.

"You made an unforgettable mark on my life. I tried to stay away, but you are too hard to resist."

"I know, I feel the same way about you."

Before either knew what was happening, his lips claimed hers, and he was instantly lost in the depths of her allure. He had no restraint when it came to this woman. He always wanted, no needed, more of her.

As the kiss became fervent, he reminded himself that if he had any decency left, he would stop. He was hanging on by a mere thread, and when her hands encircled his neck, he lost complete control.

- - - - - - - - ● - - - - - - - - - -

Kyle's lips devoured hers; his tongue explored her mouth and his very touch was what she had wanted all day. She could not seem to help herself whenever she was near him.

She wanted to tell him how she felt, but another part of her kept telling her not to get involved with another man. Her life was already complicated enough.

Yet, she could not seem to get his touch out of her mind. The flame he lit burnt hot in her very core.

He reluctantly ended the kiss, "We can't do this right now, no matter how much I want to."

Those words helped confirm what Lexi had known all along in her heart. She wanted to spend the rest of her life with him. He brought sunshine to her day. He had captured her heart.

Chapter 45

Lexi jerked awake and blinked at the daylight streaming through the windows. She sighed and waited for the profound ache of loss to leave her. The realization that Bennett was gone became almost too much to bear.

There had been so many times during the divorce that she wished him various extents of misery, but she never once imagined death. She became used to the idea of being a divorced woman, but not once did she consider the loneliness of being a surviving spouse in death.

A part of her had hoped Bennett would change his mind about their child and now, her child would never know the man who brought him life. Her heart ached for not only her child, but April's child, as well. Neither child would ever know their father.

As she tried to make herself comfortable in the front seat of Kyle's car, she prayed she could make it to the funeral home without getting sick. Kyle squeezed her hand, "Are you sure that you want to go? You don't look well at all."

She nodded and swallowed hard. She tried to find reasoning in all of this. Bennett was only forty-two, not an age where you expected a man to drop dead from a heart attack. With him being so fit, she never expected him to have heart problems.

She ran a hand over her belly and smoothed the material of the dress as she tried to calm her nerves.

Her heart broke when she walked into the funeral home and saw April crying. If this had happened several months ago, that would be her up there. She was thankful that the separation and divorce had given her emotional distance from Bennett. Still, she could not help but look at the women here to pay their condolences and wondered how many slept with her husband while they were married.

Walking up to the coffin, the sweet smell of flowers assaulted her senses, causing her stomach to roll. Her arrival caused quite a stir; as she made her way to the front, heads began to turn, and whispers followed her steps.

Gary Daigle, Bennett's father, stood next to April greeting the visitors. When he saw Lexi, he offered her a warm smile and took her hands in his, "Thank you for coming, Lexi. I was afraid that you wouldn't show."

She rubbed her stomach, "He may have been my ex-husband, but he was also my child's father."

"I'm sorry for the way my son and I have treated you. We behaved dreadfully. It is too late for Bennett to make amends, but I want to make amends."

Lexi looked at him in surprise, unsure of the right words, "Mr. Daigle, I would love a fresh start between us." Lovingly rubbing her stomach, "After all, I am carrying your grandchild."

Teary eyed, "Thank you, my dear."

Lexi was surprised to find that the service was extremely short. Bennett's family were devout Catholics, but there was no priest for his service, which she found strange. Then, as the eulogy was read, Lexi had to choke back tears as Bennett's life was recounted. Not once was their marriage mentioned. It was as if no one felt her life with Bennett deserved recognition.

Next would be the graveside service at the cemetery. As the final hymn played, visitors lined up to file past the closed casket to pay their last respects. As Lexi made her way past April, a shudder went down her spine. Even though the woman's face was immobile, her eyes were practically shooting fire.

Without warning, April stood up and pointed at Lexi, "Get out! I don't want you here."

Kyle stepped in front of Lexi to keep April from lunging at her. Lexi wondered why April freaked out. Not wanting to find out, Kyle and she hastily left the funeral home.

Once in the car, Kyle asked, "I take it we aren't going to the graveside service?"

Lexi shook her head, "You can drop me off at the house. He was your friend, too; you should go, but I won't be welcomed there."

"I tell you what, why don't we go get a bite to eat?"

"I guess we can do that."

Chapter 46

Lexi and Kyle were enjoying a peaceful dinner when April walked into the restaurant. As soon as she saw the couple, she stormed over to their table and glared at Lexi. A hysterical April pointed at Lexi accusingly, "You killed him! You killed my Bennett!"

Lexi looked at the crazed woman and said, "You need to calm down. I did no such thing."

"Yes, yes you did. You caused a heart attack with all the stress you put on Bennett lately. He would still be here if you hadn't gotten pregnant."

There was so much she wanted to tell the woman, but now was not the time. She was causing a big enough scene as it was. "April, you need to go home. All of the stress is not good for your baby. I did not kill Bennett, and somewhere in that brain of yours, you must know it. I implore you to see reason."

April glared at Lexi, "If you would have done as Bennett told you to, everything would've been fine. Why couldn't you have given your baby up for adoption so that we could have a happy life?"

Lexi scowled at the woman, "Why couldn't Bennett keep that sausage of his in his pants. If he would not have fooled around while we were married, perhaps he would not have had a heart attack. You can't blame his stress on me. He did all of this to himself."

Huffing, "You are an incorrigible woman. No wonder Bennett cheated on you."

Kyle stood up and walked over to April, "Why don't you go home for now April?"

As he ushered her to the front door, Lexi hoped that she did not return. As Lexi looked around, she groaned. Everyone in the restaurant had been watching the drama unfold. It would be all over town in an hour that April stormed in here, accusing Lexi of killing Bennett. It was bad enough that everyone was already talking about Bennett and his infidelities and getting another woman knocked up, now this. Would it ever end?

Chapter 47

Kyle handed Lexi a gift, "This is for you. Something I think you might want to wear today, while we go for a ride."

Lexi opened the gift and saw a gorgeous emerald green maternity dress, "I have enough clothes, I didn't need anything else."

Kyle helped her up from the chair and pushed her toward the room, "Go get dressed. I'm getting you out of this house for a little while. We are going for a ride."

Lexi argued, "I could have worn something that I already had."

"Nonsense, I have something special planned." Pushing her towards the door, he told her, "Now, go get dressed."

As Lexi changed and freshened her makeup, she wondered what Kyle had planned for today. Once she was dressed, she stepped out of the room, "Okay, I am ready to go if you are. But, I don't want to stay gone long. I'm kind of tired today."

Kyle gave her a grin, "Oh, I have a feeling that once you get some fresh air you will start to feel better."

He helped her out to the car, and they drove away from his house. As they continued their drive, Lexi asked, "So are you going to give me any hint as to where we are going?"

"No, you have the wait and find out."

As they got closer to her house, she glanced at him suspiciously and asked, "Why are we going back to my house? We stopped by yesterday to make sure everything was okay."

"Just enjoy the ride."

As they made it closer to her house, Lexi noticed all the vehicles parked on the street. She looked at Kyle bewildered, "What did you do? Why are there so many people at my house?"

Kyle raised his hands, as if in surrender, "I promise, this was not me. I'm just the chauffeur."

Lexi was not sure what was going on, but she knew something was up. Once parked, Kyle helped her out of the car and escorted her to her house. Once at the door, an excited Janie opened the door. "It's about time you got here." She looked at Kyle. "I thought you had failed miserably getting Lexi out of the house."

"Someone took their time getting dressed."

Lexi shrugged her shoulders, "I thought we were going for a ride. He didn't let on that he had other plans." She raised her eyebrows as she asked Janie, "Did you plan this?"

Janie smiled, "No, I had nothing to do with the actual planning," pulling Lexi inside, "but wait until you see what is going on."

Lexi walked into her house to find it decorated in hues of yellow and green baby shower decorations. There were elephants, monkeys, and even giraffes on some of the decorations. Lexi's mom rushed over to her daughter and gave her a hug, "It's about time you got here. I've been counting the minutes until you arrived."

Lexi looked at her mom and asked, "You did this?"

Smiling, "Guilty. I wanted to make up for all the difficulties I've given you lately. I wanted to show you that I was happy you are having a baby, and that I'm thrilled to be a grandparent again. I never doubted for one minute that you wouldn't love this child." Kissing her daughter on the cheek, "And you will be a great mother."

Kyle looked at the women and stated, "Okay ladies, I'm going to let you enjoy your day. Janie, what time would you like me to come back and pick up Lexi?"

Janie told Kyle, "I'll bring her back later on when we're done."

Lexi's mom looked at them, "Or, if she wants to spend the night here, I can stay and take care of her tonight."

After Kyle left, her mom pulled Lexi into the living room, "Now, let's get this baby shower started."

Lexi noticed that her friends and family were here, all with gifts. "Oh my, I can't thank you all enough for coming. I am so surprised and so excited." Lexi never even considered having a baby shower. She had already ordered most of the big items, and figured she would wait until closer to her due date before purchasing the smaller items.

Christi walked over and gave her friend a hug, "Well, you made it difficult for us to buy you anything. You have most of the big items."

Over the next hour, they played games, ate goodies, and opened gifts. As her company left, Janie and her mom informed her, "We have one more surprise for you."

The two women led Lexi to the nursery and opened the door. "We know that you haven't had time to finish the nursery, so we wanted to make sure you didn't have that to worry with."

Lexi looked at the room and felt overwhelmed with emotions. The crib now had sheets and a blanket. The changing table had diapers, baby necessities, and the changing pad. "I can't thank you both enough for all of this." Unable to fight the tears of joy any longer, Lexi cried as she gave each woman a hug.

Chapter 48

Lexi was surprised to see a letter addressed to her in today's mail. She could not remember the last time she had received a personal letter in the mail, usually, everyone tended to send emails nowadays.

Curious, she opened the letter,

"Dear Lexi,

I didn't have the courage to talk to you face-to-face. I have behaved horribly these last few months, and would completely understand if you never wanted to talk to me again. However, if you can find it in your heart to forgive me, I would appreciate it.

As the birth of my baby gets closer, I am beginning to realize how important family is. Only, my family has chosen to disown me. They are ashamed that my child was not only conceived out of wedlock, but that my pregnancy came about out of an affair with a married man that I then married after having ruined his.

Bennett's death hit me hard. I never thought, or took into consideration, how you felt though.

April"

Lexi was stunned by the letter. April had been so cruel and hateful that it was difficult for her to forgive her. While Bennett refused to acknowledge the child he had conceived with Lexi, at least she had her family support. Without their love and support, this pregnancy would have been a challenge. A part of her wanted to feel sympathy for April and dealing with the pregnancy by herself.

- - - - - - ●●●●●●●● ● ● ● - - -

Kyle came home to find Lexi asleep on his couch. She lay on her right side, her hand beneath her cheek. Her shoes were on the floor, leaving her feet exposed in colorfully striped socks. Her cheeks were flushed and her lips slightly parted. Long lashes framed her fair cheeks. As he moved closer to her, he frowned. Was there a trace of tears on her face? Had she been crying?

He shifted his weight uncomfortably, unsure what to do. Should he wake her? Should he let her sleep?

Before he could make up his mind, Lexi stirred. "I'm sorry, Kyle. I must have fallen asleep."

"I didn't want to wake you. You look so peaceful. Besides, your body was probably telling you that you needed the sleep."

He studied her suspiciously puffy eyelids. In a vaguely concerned tone, "Is everything okay?"

She wiped nonchalantly at her cheeks, as if removing signs of sleep rather than any hint of tears. She smiled, but he had the distinct impression something was wrong. For one thing, she was playing with her hair, unconsciously twisting it around her finger. A nervous habit she'd had since childhood.

"Oh, sure. I must've been sleeping hard."

Something was troubling her, and he hoped she would tell him if and when she was ready.

- - - - - - - ● - - - - - - - -

Lexi wondered if she should show Kyle the letter. No, perhaps she should wait before she mentioned it.

She smoothed her tousled hair with one hand and looked at Kyle, "Have you eaten?"

"No, not yet."

Pushing him toward the kitchen, "Good, I made us gumbo."

Kyle gave her a suspicious look, "You made gumbo?" Shaking his head back and forth, "I'm not sure I'm ready to be a guinea pig."

Swatting at him as he joked, "I've already tried it; I'm not going to use you as my guinea pig."

Chapter 49

Kyle anxiously waited for Lexi to come down the stairs; he had never been this nervous. He prayed that everything went well tonight. He had charted out the route earlier with his captain. If Lexi became uncomfortable with the rocking of the boat on the water, they could head back in, but if she was enjoying herself, they could head out for deeper water. The newest boat he purchased, a seventy-two foot Viking Motor Yacht, had been well customized. Even though it was built in 1990, it had been elegantly furnished and well-equipped. She had magnificent staterooms, a four head layout, and a day head on the deck. There was a spacious full beam aft Master Stateroom and two VIP Staterooms forward with King and Queen berths. The previous owners recently completed her very extensive and costly custom refit.

He made sure the staterooms were thoroughly cleaned just in case they spent the night and Lexi wanted her own room. Not wishing to force any issues on her, but he prayed that she joined him in the master stateroom.

- - - - - - - - - - - - - - - -

Lexi tried to get dressed as fast as she could, but lately, the task had become quite cumbersome. She had two weeks left in this pregnancy and could not wait. Kyle insisted they eat dinner on his new boat. The owner of the Viking tried to squeeze out a few more dollars from Kyle, but in the end, Kyle proved to him that if he didn't purchase this particular boat it wouldn't be the end of the world.

When she saw the excitement in his eyes, she could not find it in her heart to tell him that she was not up to it. Besides, a nice, relaxing night on the water may be just what she needed. The baby had been energetic today; flipping and kicking more than usual.

As soon as Kyle saw her in the doorway, he smiled over at her. He walked over, sweeping her into his arms and kissed her before asking, "Are you ready for supper?"

She held out her hand, "Believe it or not, I am famished. I don't understand why you wanted us to get dressed up though."

"You deserve a nice supper. I thought getting dressed up might put a smile on your face is all. Besides, we need to christen the boat for good luck."

She stood up on her tiptoes and kissed him, "You may be right, but it is difficult for me to get dressed right now."

She assumed they would eat a simple meal. Stepping on the deck of the boat, she was surprised to see that he took the time to have the whole yacht transformed for tonight. This had to be the most romantic setting she had ever seen. There were red, pink and white roses throughout, as well as candlelight. There was also romantic music being played in the background. It was almost as if a small orchestra was playing just for them. She smiled up at him, "You did this?"

He smiled down at her, "I had a little help."

As he helped her into a chair, a waiter appeared with a plate of appetizers. The aroma of the BBQ shrimp was too tantalizing to resist. No matter how many times she made this at home, it never came out this good. To her, this was sunshine on a plate.

As they dined on the appetizer, they made general conversation about their day. It was not long before the waiter came in to take away the appetizer dishes and brought out the main entrée. At first, she was not sure she had room for any more food until she saw what he had planned.

She smiled over at him, "I may have to let you do my ordering from now on. This is an exquisite meal."

He reached over and squeezed her hand, "I want you to enjoy yourself before the baby comes. You deserve to be pampered."

As she looked over the main course, she was not sure what she wanted to dive into first. The pan seared salmon topped with a lump crab sauce or bacon wrapped asparagus served over garlic herb butter pasta.

She told him, "I'm not sure who enjoys the meal more, me or the baby."

She was in absolute heaven over the exquisitely prepared salmon that the chef had seasoned and cooked to perfection. The tender salmon flaked beautifully with the touch of her fork.

She smiled in pleasure as dessert was served. It was a decadent double chocolate cake, with creamy white chocolate mousse filling, and a delicious chocolate ganache frosting. This was chocolate heaven to her and utterly sinful.

After they had finished eating, Kyle stood up, holding out his hand to her and asked, "Would you care to dance? Or would you rather head back to the dock?"

"I'm not ready for the night to end."

After he had instructed the captain to move the yacht into deeper waters, he swept Lexi into his arms.

She immediately fell into his embrace, not wanting to miss the chance to have those strong arms of his wrapped around her. Being in his arms was heaven and his warm embrace caused a wonderful mix of excitement and contentment. Even with her expanding stomach, they managed to move gracefully across the floor.

She felt like a fairytale princess as they moved in perfect synchronization, floating to the melody. Each step was in tune with the music and each other. She reminded herself that this was only a dance, nothing more. But for a moment, just the tiniest moment, she imagined what it would be like if they were a couple. She wished that she could forget her past, mend her broken heart and fall in love.

Instead, she was too afraid to trust again. She was wary of commitment by others.

Of course, she was just letting her mind wander. Kyle had no intentions of wooing her. She was nine months pregnant and in no position to have anybody woo her. Besides, no man in his right mind wanted to get involved with her now.

He shifted her body to where she was closer to him and kissed her deeply. She felt his tongue slip inside her mouth. His lips felt like silk against hers. His kiss ignited something deep inside of her.

Once the dance was over, he took a tiny black box out of his pocket. She watched in utter surprise as he bent on one knee. She was not sure if this was even real, "Lexi, I want to marry you before the baby is born. We can apply for our marriage license now and have a small wedding this weekend. I desperately want you and this child in my life. You will both have the best in life. What can be better than parents who mean the world to each other? Who love each other with all their hearts? When we say 'I do' it will be until death do us part. My life is nothing without you. You are my whole world. You have my heart in your hands. I will cherish you always."

Swelling tears glistened in her eyes. She bent down as dread crept deep into her heart, "I love you with all my heart, but marriage scares me."

"I cannot erase what Bennett has done, but you should know that I am not Bennett." Tilting her chin, he stared into her eyes as he said, "Lexi, I want to grow old with you."

She stared intently at the two-carat emerald cut diamond ring as it shined up at her from its black velvet cushion. The reality of what this ring meant sank in. Kyle wanted both her and the baby. He was ready to make a lifelong commitment to not only her, but her child also. This was not a spur of the moment decision. He took the time and bought a ring especially for her.

As if sensing her hesitation, "I am a slave to your heart. I have been yours for a long time now, cher."

"What happens once we are married and you find fault with all my inadequacies?"

"Ah honey, I love you just the way you are. We have been friends for so long. I have seen all you have to offer." Looking into her eyes, he admitted, "When Bennett proposed to you, I thought I lost out on my chance. I feared that since you were one of my best friends I should not act on my feelings. When you and

Bennett divorced, the feelings I had buried surfaced once more. What you consider your shortcomings are the things that I find endearing. I like that we are opposites. We are like the yen and yang, oil and water; yet, somehow when we come together, the chemistry is unbelievable."

She looked at the ring once more. Nothing in his expression told her he had any doubts. He took a moment just looking at her, "I won't disappoint you, Lexi. You are an amazing person. I am continually blown away by your strength and the love you have for the child you are carrying. I would be a lucky man if you made me your husband. I would be honored to share my life with you."

She looked at the man kneeling here asking her to be his wife. When she looked into his eyes, she could see them twinkling with love for her. The air was thick with sexual tension. She had difficulty breathing being so close to him.

Could she trust her heart to another man? Bennett promised a lifelong commitment, and he was out of her life now. Before his death, he had thrown the most insulting blow to her by having his parental rights terminated to his unborn child. Bennett never wanted to be part of their child's life; yet, this man did.

Kyle stood and held Lexi's trembling hands in his, "I love you Lexi with all my heart," he whispered against her lips sending a shudder of desire straight to the very core of her being. She struggled futilely to hold on to the last threads of logic, but when his lips touched hers, all her arguments were lost. Her heart drummed wildly as he pulled her into his warm embrace. As his kiss deepened, she knew that this was indeed the man she wanted to spend the rest of her life with. This was the man she wanted to grow old with. This was the man she wanted to raise her children with. He whispered in her ear, "I know you. Stop over thinking this and just feel."

She swallowed nervously as equal parts of trepidation and anticipation filled her. Taking a deep breath, she looked deep into his eyes. "Yes, Kyle, my love, I will be your wife."

"You have made me the happiest man on this planet. I will love you and this child with all of my heart."

He kissed her with an all-consuming kiss, touching her very soul. Her emotions spilled out more compassionately than she anticipated. It soon built to a very passionate crescendo. He picked up the ring, slipped it onto her finger, and looked at the ring he specifically chose for this woman. With tears in her eyes, she kissed him once more.

His hands moved over her body, sending a trail of goosebumps in their wake. She wrapped her arms around his neck as the kiss deepened. She arched against him as his lips trailed a blaze of hot, wanton kisses down her neck.

She felt his body's growing eagerness against her stomach as he groaned deeply. He captured her mouth once more with so much intensity that she lost her breath. She looked into his eyes to find that they were clouded with passion. "I can't wait to make you my wife."

As they stood together on the deck of the boat watching the moonlight glitter against the waves, Lexi knew in her heart that she had made the right decision.

Chapter 50

By Saturday afternoon, Lexi found herself pacing the bedroom. They arranged to have a wedding at Kyle's house. It would be a simple outdoor wedding with only a few of their closest friends and family members present. Lexi's parents were here even though they were both surprised to hear about the upcoming wedding.

As she thought back to everything that happened this past year, she was surprised by how much her life had changed. Before his death, Bennett turned his life's mission into making her life miserable. He even accused them of having an affair behind his back. Lexi wanted to force Bennett into a DNA test to confirm the paternity of the child, but Kyle asked her to let it be. When that did not get the reaction Bennett wanted, he then severed his parental rights, which perhaps was for the best. Kyle would be a better father to this baby than Bennett ever would. It sickened her to think that Bennett wanted her to kill a child who was a part of him.

She grimaced as she looked in the mirror at her reflection once more. She looked like a giant marshmallow. Although the dress was an antique white and lace gown; she did not feel the least bit sexy. Yet, she should not expect to look breathtaking when she was nine months pregnant.

As they stood together with her clutching her bouquet of flowers, listening to the pastor offer words of advice on marriage, she thought back to her first wedding. That minister also talked about couples growing old together and weathering the ups and downs of life. Look how well that turned out for her. As if sensing her thoughts, Kyle squeezed her hand. As she looked into his eyes, she came to the realization that he was nothing like Bennett. This man in front of her was offering his heart not only to her, but also her unborn child. He was willing to take the two of them and wrap them each in his love's embrace.

As they said their vows, the rings were handed to each of them. Once done, the pastor looked at Kyle, "You may now kiss your bride."

"I do love you, Mrs. Kyle DuPont, with all my heart."

Smiling, she reaffirmed her love, "As I love you, my husband."

As they greeted their friends and family, it was strange to find that she was now Mrs. Kyle DuPont. Every time she saw the ring on her finger, her heart swelled with love.

As everyone talked and laughed, Lexi found a chair to sit on just for a bit. The last few days were impossibly busy as she made sure everything in her office was taken care of for her maternity leave. In a few short weeks, she would be taking several weeks off as she prepared for the arrival of the baby.

She also had moved everything out of her house and gave her landlord notice. It had been bittersweet moving out of the house. She would miss it to a certain degree since it was where she had imagined raising her baby.

Doctor's appointments and childbirth classes had also kept her busy. She was elated when Kyle took time out of his busy schedule to attend every appointment and class with her.

As she watched her husband walk over to her, she felt a tightening in her stomach. As he leaned down and kissed her on the lips, she felt another quick tightening.

Just as she was about to stand up, a contraction gripped her stomach, nothing unbearable but breath catching. Kyle watched her with intent eyes, "You had a contraction didn't you?"

Before she could answer, another contraction hit her. She bit her lip to get through this one.

She tried to calm him down, "It is nothing to worry about just yet. I have had a few, and they are rather far apart." She ran a caring thumb along his brow line, smoothing away the worry. "Stop worrying. You are going to get permanent wrinkles in your forehead."

Without warning, the sharp pains began, and the pressure became unbearable. Before she had time to think, a gush of water came rushing out.

"I think my water just broke."

"We have to get you to the hospital."

She nodded her head in agreement, her contractions were now closer together and sitting became almost unbearable. By the time they made it to the car, their wedding guests knew she was in labor.

As Kyle made good time to the hospital; he never once let go of her hand. She prayed they made it in time as she was consumed by the pain of another contraction.

Once they walked inside, she was greeted by a nurse with a wheelchair at the emergency room entrance. Kyle looked at Lexi and informed her, "I called ahead to let them know we were on our way."

Dr. Allen was waiting for her in the room, "Well, young lady, it looks as if you are having a very busy day. You could have a wedding and birth on the same day." As he arranged her legs in the stirrups, he confirmed what she already knew, "You are getting ready to have this baby. You are nine centimeters dilated."

Shocked, Lexi looked at him, "That is fast isn't it?"

"Well, this baby is anxious to make its entrance into the world."

Kyle smiled down at her, "Maybe the baby wanted to be at the wedding?"

"I only wish I had a chance to eat a piece of that wedding cake. I thought about it all day. On top of that, we won't have a chance for a honeymoon now."

Kyle kissed her, "I am sure there will be plenty of time for a honeymoon. My mother can't wait to get her hands on this grandchild of hers."

As she prepared to give birth, it finally hit her that she was married to Kyle. For better or worse, in sickness and health, he was her husband. In her heart, she knew when Kyle said those vows he meant every word of them.

Tears of joy filled her eyes. Until now, she always doubted whether he intended to stay, but now she realized that he would be devoted entirely to his new family. She reached out and touched Kyle's face lovingly. He bent down and kissed her just as another contraction hit. This one had been the worst yet, and she gripped his hand tightly.

He reminded her, "Just remember to breathe." He started breathing as they were instructed in the birth classes. With each deep breath, she found that it helped, but she still refused to let go of his hand. His other hand stroked her hair as his eyes filled with concern for her.

For the next several minutes, she concentrated on her breathing as the contractions moved closer together. With each contraction, she knew that she was one step closer to seeing her baby. She could not wait to see what this little person growing inside of her these last nine months looked like.

As exhaustion took its toll on her body, Dr. Allen walked in with concern showing on his face. "We are going to give you an IV to help with your fluids. The baby's heartbeat is dropping. I thought at the rate you were dilating you would have delivered by now, but this child of yours has a mind of its own."

Kyle watched in dismay, "Will they be okay?"

Dr. Allen continued his examination of her as he informed the two of them, "We have to watch the two of you carefully to make sure the baby isn't going into distress. I will have an ultrasound machine brought in to make sure everything is okay. The baby may be larger than we anticipated and has become stuck in her pelvic opening. It could also be that he turned again and wants to come into this world breech."

Before leaving the room, Dr. Allen gave her arm a comforting pat. She closed her eyes as the tears threatened to spill. She looked at Kyle, "I am worried about the baby. I have tried so hard to do all the right things and now to have something go wrong."

He kissed her reassuringly, "You are in some of the best hands around. Dr. Allen will do everything in his power to deliver a healthy baby."

Just as another contraction hit, the anesthesiologist came in to administer an epidural. After that, the pains gradually decreased. Dr. Allen came back in quickly, "The fluids are not helping. We have to do an emergency C-section. Your baby's heart rate is dropping faster than I would like."

Lexi gripped Kyle's hand as tears fell, "Please, just make sure that the baby is fine."

Before she had time to prepare her mind for the C-section, she was wheeled into the operating room. Everything was a blur as her body was draped and prepared for the surgery. Kyle continued to offer words of encouragement, "Just think it won't be long now before you can meet this baby. Soon, we will find out if we have a son or daughter."

Dr. Allen called out, "Okay, are you ready to greet this baby?" Dr. Allen motioned for Kyle to come watch as the baby was brought into this world. In a few short seconds, it was over, and the silence in the room was filled with the loud cry of a baby.

As tears streamed down her face, Kyle carried the baby to his mother, "He is perfect Lexi. You have a son." As she looked at her child, she could not help but think today was the most incredible day of her life. As the nurse took the baby from Kyle's hands, alarms filled the room. Dr. Allen and Kyle watched as Lexi's face paled fast. Suddenly, a large amount of blood flowed to the floor.

Dr. Allen ordered the nurse, "You need to get him out of here." As Kyle was rushed out the door, he could hear the doctor barking orders to the rest of the staff. The nurse took Kyle into the nursery, "Let's get this baby cleaned up. You can give him his first bath and bottle."

- - - - - - - - ● - - - - - - - -

As Kyle listened to the words coming out of the nurse's mouth, he looked back in the operating room and worried about Lexi. "Is she going to be okay?"

"As soon as I know something, you will be the first to find out. I promise you she is in the best of hands."

In the room, the nurse suctioned and let Kyle help her clean the baby. Afterward, she weighed and measured him, "Your son is a healthy eight pounds and nine ounces. He will also be a tall little boy. He is nineteen inches long." As she swaddled him in a blanket, she asked, "Have you decided on a name yet?"

Kyle shook his head, "I don't think Lexi has thought of names. She said that as soon as she saw the baby she would know what to name it."

The nurse nodded her head, "Well then, why don't you introduce this little guy to everyone anxiously waiting to meet him while I go check on your wife?"

As he walked to the waiting room, he looked back at the nurse and said sadly, "That woman in there is my whole life. I just got her back and I can't lose her now." Fighting back the tears, "She hasn't even met her son."

The nurse looked at him with sympathy, "I completely understand. She is in excellent hands. Dr. Allen will do everything he can to make sure that she meets her son."

- - - - - - - - - ● - - - - - - - - -

As Kyle made his way to the waiting room, he looked at the beautiful baby he was holding. This little boy had a full head of black hair, just like his father, but his face was reminiscent of his mother. Even the expressions on his face while looking up at Kyle reminded him of Lexi.

While he waited to hear what was happening with her, his stomach was in knots as he thought about what could be wrong. The longer it was before the nurse came out with news, the more he worried that the news was not good.

As soon as he opened the doors, the grandparents surrounded the baby. Kyle's mother kissed the baby's forehead, "Oh my, he is the best looking baby that I have ever seen."

Lexi's mom looked at the baby with tears in her eyes, "He looks just like Lexi. I can't believe that my baby has a baby."

Lexi's dad asked, "How is Lexi? When can we see her?"

Kyle swallowed back the fear building in his voice, "There were complications with the delivery. We should hear something soon though."

Lexi's mom swooned as her husband caught her, "Complications? What do you mean complications?"

As Kyle took the baby back in his arms, "I am not sure yet. I haven't been told much, just that they needed to tend to Lexi while I bonded with the baby."

He could not get the picture of all the blood and her pale face out of his mind. He had never been this scared.

Kyle did not want to remember today as his wedding day, the birth of his son, and the death of his wife. It would be too much to take. He could not get over how life could change in a heartbeat. Just when he found love, it could be snatched from him.

As soon as the nurse walked into the waiting room, he knew that the news was not good. The nurse carefully took the baby from him, "I will take him back to the nursery."

Nodding his head, he tried to hold back the tears as he entered the room, unsure if he would be able to keep it together. One look at Lexi's face and his whole world crumbled in front of him. He took her hand in his as he talked to her, "You always know how to do things with a flare don't you, my love. Your baby, our baby, is perfect. He has the blackest hair I have ever seen. The biggest eyes and sweetest face you could ever imagine. He looks so much like you; it is unbelievable. I promise you that I will do right by him. I will be the best father that a boy could ask for." Kyle had to stop and dry the tears from his face before he could continue. This was the most heartbreaking conversation he had ever had and wished he wasn't even having it. Lexi was supposed to be alert and breast feeding their child. Instead, he was describing her baby to her while she was in the ICU room fighting for her life. The doctor stopped the bleeding, and now all they could do was wait.

After leaving the room, he walked to the tiny chapel in the hospital. Dropping to his knees, he prayed. He was unable to control the tears flowing freely from his eyes. He was not sure he could survive this heartache, but there was a child now, another living person whose life depended on him.

- -

Kyle held his son, Alex James DuPont, in one arm, and the other hand carried a bouquet of Lexi's favorite flowers, white roses with blood red on the edges. The color still reminded him of all the blood Lexi lost to deliver their son. Kyle chose the name Alex after the woman who gave him life; the woman who loved him more than anything on this earth.

The church was silent as Kyle made his way to the front altar. Even Alex must have realized this was a time to be quiet as he just looked up into his dad's face with a somber expression.

Little Alex was only a week old; yet, Kyle could not imagine his life without him in it. His life changed drastically this last week.

As Kyle braced himself for today's church service, he adjusted the christening gown on Alex before handing the child to the anxiously awaiting arms.

- - - - - - - - - - - - - - - - - - - -

Lexi smiled at her child with tears in her eyes. It had been a rough week, but the end was worth it. She would do it all again, too, even if Kyle was wary of having another child. They were lucky that Dr. Allen could save her uterus. At first, he feared he would have to do a complete hysterectomy, but he warned her that if she did decide to have another child they would have to be extremely careful. This could happen again and the next time, she may need a hysterectomy. If it meant giving Kyle a child of his own, it would be worth it.

After Alex's baptism, he let them know it was time to eat. Lexi found a quiet place where she could feed her son before heading back home. No sooner than he clamped onto her breast he let out a soft little moan. He closed his eyes and smacked loudly.

Kyle walked up to the two of them, "It looks like our son is a real chowhound."

Smiling, she nodded, "He is a growing boy after all. I am surprised at his urgency with each feeding. It is as if he can't seem to get enough." Lexi had just finished feeding Alex when she felt a gentle tap on her shoulder. She was surprised to see Gary Daigle standing beside her, looking rather uncertain. "I know how Bennett felt about this child; he made no qualms about hiding his feelings. I also know how my wife treated you while she was alive, but as I had told you at Bennett's funeral, I am hoping you will still allow me to be a part of his child's life?"

She looked up at him with tears in her eyes, and a soft smile. "And as I told you, and I meant it, I would like that very much."

"May I please hold my grandson?"

Lexi handed Alex to his grandfather, "This child will be well loved with all of his grandparents."

Kyle placed his hand on her back as he watched Gary holding Alex, "And very spoiled."

As he held his grandson, he looked at Lexi and Kyle. There was a sadness in her father-in-law's eyes as he said, "Cherish your baby. Hold on to every precious moment, because it can be gone before you know it."

His words shook Lexi. She felt a sharp ache at his loss, even though Bennett had caused her so much pain. He had to go through the rest of his life knowing that his son was dead. Their precious moments together were gone forever.

Nothing Lexi could say or do would ease that pain.

Epilogue

"Dear April,

The birth of Alex has made me truly understand the importance of family. While it is difficult for me to forgive everything that has happened, I would like to try. Our children do share the same father and are half-brothers. It would be unfair of me to keep Alex from knowing his sibling.

When you are ready to meet in person, I will be ready.

Lexi"

Now it would be up to April to make the next move.

www.ingramcontent.com/pod-product-compliance
Lightning Source LLC
Chambersburg PA
CBHW070756190726
48292CB00002B/546